My Father, The Assassin

A Romantic Thriller

Second Addition

By June Finnigan

Copyright ©2009 – June Finnigan

Registration Number: 923174848

ISBN-10: 1508698686

ISBN-13: 9781508698685

Dedication

To Paul for his ceaseless patience, encouragement and love.

To Gisella

Amore

June xp

(signature)

My Father, The Assassin

Second Addition

By June Finnigan

Prologue

My father, *George Worme*, was born in 1921 the only son of Lora, a Romany gypsy; it was rumoured that she had had a brief affair with an army captain, stationed at a nearby camp in Yorkshire. George's uncle, Seth, confronted the Captain but was badly beaten for his trouble, so the Gypsies decided to move on and put the affair behind them.

George was a precocious little lad and the women of the tribe adored his black curly hair, mischievous dark eyes, and wicked smile. Uncle Seth was a skilled poacher and wanted to bring the little lad up as his own, so he gave the boy his first rifle at the age of six. George blasted a hole in the head of his first deer at the age of eight and never looked back. Anything that moved was in danger of George's obsession with guns.

He shot his first man when he was twelve. Some said that George had mistaken the victim for a deer or wild pig; others said that as the man was a local squire, trying to get the gypsies off his land, George had murdered him. Either way, the tribe moved on again. When George was thirteen, the gypsies arrived in Devon and set up camp just outside Exeter. Lora was taken ill and she and George were taken to the local hospital. There is no record of the severity of her illness, but the tribe was forced to move on again, and left her and George behind.

A nurse took pity on them and when Lora was well, she took them into her own home. Lora cleaned, cooked, sewed, and caught the eye of the nurse's brother Bill. She and Bill were married and moved into a little terraced house south of the river in Exeter. George refused to go to school and wondered the streets a lot, petty thieving and looking for fights. As he still had his rifle, Bill thought it might focus the lad if he joined the local shooting club. By the age of fifteen, George had gone into business moving black market goods from a lock-up by the river. He managed to obtain almost anything and mostly by foul means. At the shooting club, he attracted the attention of a Royal Marine Officer who persuaded George to enlist; however, he failed the medical because his left arm was shrivelled. This handicap had never bothered George, but it bothered the recruiting officers, however, they did take note of his skill as a sharp shooter.

My mother, **Monique de Worthy**, was born in 1924, the only daughter of wealthy middle class parents. She was pretty, a natural blond and had eyes the colour of a summer sky. Her mother, Nelly, was a direct descendant of Henry 1st, on the female side, and had inherited a certain amount of wealth. Nelly enjoyed travelling in Europe and was a fine painter of watercolours. Monique's father, Henry, was a restorer of fine art and owned a business in Exeter, where his skills demanded high fees. Monique's childhood was reasonably happy and she did not want for anything. The family was strict Methodist and most of Monique's friends were children of churchgoers.

The family owned a grand Edwardian villa north of the river in Exeter. Monique was privately educated and went on to win school certificates in several subjects and entry to the University of Exeter, where she studied history and art. She also played cricket and was considered a good all-rounder. At eighteen, she met the man who was to become her fiancé. Captain John Hamilton was with the Royal Fusiliers and of good breeding stock, as his parents owned land in Somerset and were friends with royalty. In 1942, he was killed in action so Monique decided to devote her time to studying. Exeter University became her second home and she made many new interesting friends.

Prince Abdullah of Malaysia was also born in 1924. His father, a Sultan, held high office in government and owned property and land around Kuala Lumpur. The nineteen twenties and thirties were periods of unrest in the region and Abdullah was kept safely under his mother's wing until his early teens. He was small for his age, good-looking and intelligent. At the age of six, his parents employed an English private tutor to educate him in English, history and the arts. She was quite young and attractive, so when the Prince lost his virginity to her at the age of thirteen, he considered it all part of his education.

At sixteen, the Prince was sent to military school in England. The change of lifestyle was a complete shock, but in time, he learnt the art of war and threw himself into socialising with his fellow trainee officers. At eighteen, his father decided that his son would be safer away from the war zone, and instructed him to stay in England. He was enrolled into Exeter University and, like Monique, began to study history and the arts.

Over the next few years, fate would bring *George, Monique* and *Abdullah* together. Their lives would become irreversibly joined, like the links of a barbed wire fence. A little while later, I would enter the world, crying, puking in my mother's arms and oblivious to the black cloud of doom that waited to smother us.

Welcome to my world. My name is *Joanna Wilde*.

Chapter One

Early July 1995, Devonshire, England

This incredible life changing experience, which I am about to share with you, began with the unexpected slow purr of a car engine cruising down the lane to my house. I had lived here, in my Devon farmhouse, for nearly two years, deliberately isolated and alone, with Dippy the black Labrador. The only sounds to penetrate our peaceful existence were the call of the buzzard and the faint echoing of the Exeter to Paddington express train. In short, life had been idyllic since I had thrown aside the stress of city fund management, for a life in the countryside. I had worked bloody hard and invested well. Emma, my daughter, had left home two years earlier and I could see no reason for continuing to slog myself silly into my late-forties. The business sold quickly and the new owner moved into the London flat. Just six weeks after having made my momentous decision, I had established myself back in my home county of Devon. Memories of the late sixties and the only man I had ever loved, Dominic Francis, no longer dominated my days.

Two weeks before the arrival of the car, Emma had driven down from London to take me out for a birthday lunch and we enjoyed a nice bottle of Chianti overlooking the Exe estuary at Topsham. June was always a good month for eating by the river; the holidaymakers, known locally as grockles, were still thin on the ground. I had always loved being around boats; the cry of the seagulls and the hoot of the small cargo ships heading for the Exeter ship canal, were the most nostalgic of sounds. Emma's company too, was total pleasure. Despite my being a single mother, having her was the best decision I had ever made. She had just started her own PR business and was so entertaining; mimicking this client and that buyer. She was on the springboard of a new and exciting career and I remembered that adrenalin rush so well.

Then two weeks later, whilst enjoying a cool beer in the garden, I heard the sound of the car. A white stretch limousine was slowly coming to a halt at the bottom of my lane! I rarely had visitors and the few people that I could call true friends, had been given my ex-directory number and always telephoned first. Perhaps this driver had taken a wrong turn.

Dippy was barking furiously at a rather large oriental man in a peaked hat, who was struggling to undo the string on the garden gate! I was looking terribly scruffy and quickly ran my fingers through my hair, only to find a piece of dried bramble which tore into my hand. I rushed to the gate rubbing my hand into my jeans and tried to grab Dippy's collar, terrified that the visitor might at any minute attract a well-practised set of canines. The only way to calm Dippy was to untie the string and let this odd-looking person into the garden.

"If I invite you into the garden, the dog will stop barking and we'll be able to hear ourselves speak!" I shouted, over the din. The nervous man gingerly took a few paces forward and bowed. "Please to confirm that I am addressing Miss Joanna Wilde?" He was unable to take his eyes off Dippy, who was now circling him at a furious pace and slavering at the same time. "It depends who's asking." I responded, whilst feeling as if I were being assessed for a meeting with somebody terribly important. "If you are Miss Joanna Wilde, then His Royal Highness, Prince Abdullah of Malaysia, wishes to seek urgent audience with you."

I looked down at my feet. Apart from the whole situation seeming incredibly unreal, I was wearing muddy boots, torn jeans and an old, faded tee shirt. My fingernails were black and I had consumed three bottles of beer following an hour's strenuous digging in the vegetable patch. Dippy, much to the relief of the visitor, had finally ceased his thunderous gallop and sat panting at my side. I grabbed his collar. "Quite frankly" I gasped, still struggling with the incredulity of the situation. "Now is not a good time to meet anyone, least of all His Royal Highness Prince whatshisname!"

"It is of extreme importance that I speak with you without delay!" A small,

EL 2
Maths 1.
ICT 2

Practice:
Maths Level 1

Reservations: abo@ujclub.co.uk
Events: events@ujclub.co.uk
Telephone 020 7902 6000
www.ujclub.co.uk

white-haired Far Eastern gentleman stepped out from behind the ivy-covered wall. He wore a cream suit, with an oversized red carnation pinned to the lapel. His Italian shoes were highly polished and a pair of dark, gold-framed glasses rested on the end of his tiny nose. In contrast to his obvious affluence, his face was pinched and lined. He must have been well into his seventies and not in a very good state of health. Leaning heavily on an ivory handled walking stick, he looked intently into my eyes and I got the distinct feeling that it would definitely be in my best interest to let the little man have his say. So, my curiosity aroused and feeling not just a little vulnerable, I invited him to join me under the pergola on the old garden bench.

The Prince sat down with a sigh of relief. "You live in a beautiful, if remote place, Miss Wilde. It has proved quite difficult to track you down!" He had spoken perfect Queen's English with only a hint of Malaysian accent. Then he took two short choking breaths, removed his glasses and placed them on the wooden table beside him. "I was a friend and business associate of your father." He spread his hands on the table and took a long deep breath. "The last time I saw him was in 1969. I hired him to do a job of work for me and as usual, he did it well. However, after completing his last contract, he took something that did not belong to him. At that time, it was not possible to track him down, without drawing attention to myself. Politically, you see, this might have been suicide on my part. I had been educated at Exeter University and had many friends in England, but I could not take the risk of alerting the British authorities."

My father, connected with my father? I was dumbfounded. This had to be a mistake! My father had died in 1973, following one of his many drunken binges at the local pub. He had failed to negotiate a flight of steps, fallen on his face, and broken his neck. Not only was he a small-town drunk but an extremely unpleasant character as well. To my knowledge, he had never done anything worthwhile during his fifty odd years of wasted life. Not one person had shed a tear. For my father to have been associated with Prince Abdullah seemed plainly ridiculous. Nevertheless, I decided to humour this serious little man. I was, in any case, curious to hear more about the man who, in my view, could not possibly be my deceased father!

Chapter Two

Sitting down on a kitchen chair, I removed my wellies, and with a deep sigh placed my hot feet on the cold flagstones. Against my better judgement, I had offered the Prince and his gorilla, cold beers. Anyway, I had needed an excuse to be alone for a few minutes and to get my thoughts together. I opened the fridge and looked at the depleted stock of bottles; just enough left to cool the Prince's throat and calm my over-active mind. I placed the bottles and two glasses on a tray; no doubt the gorilla would drink straight from the bottle, then I slipped into an old pair of Jesus sandals and turned towards the kitchen door.

The Gorilla's frame more than filled the doorway. "I wish to use the bathroom, if Miss Wilde would be so kind." His politeness belied his bulk and threatening stance. I found myself smiling, amused at this apparition, and nodded towards the downstairs loo. As I stepped back into the heat of the garden, the brightness of the sun was momentarily blinding. I shaded my eyes and saw the Prince was standing, as if to show me to my seat. However, he hastily changed his mind when he saw Dippy lurching towards him. As soon as I was seated, Dippy settled in the shade of the old chestnut tree and stretched out fully. His eyes, however, remained fixed on the poor man.

"In Malaya, dogs are considered to be a delicacy," the Prince hissed. "In the west, there are more domestic dogs than children. I will never understand this strange relationship!"

At that moment, I felt an instant dislike for this bony little man. Anyone who was not a dog lover was definitely not in my address book. Out of the corner of my eye, I could see the Gorilla walking slowly and quietly back towards the car, clutching his beer bottle like an offensive weapon. I watched him weave his way between the overgrown lavenders, and finally settle down on the old stone churn shelf. Then, suddenly feeling rather impatient, I returned my attention to the Prince.

"You were about to tell me more about your connection with my father," I prompted. "Yes, Miss Wilde. But first, I would like to know why you changed your name to Wilde?" "Your question surprises me, your Highness. If you knew my father, then you must also have known his surname. Being saddled with a name like Joanna Worme was not exactly a door opener for a woman intending to embark on a high profile business career!" I snapped.

The corners of his mouth twitched as if trying to suppress laughter. I angrily reached for a beer bottle and replenished my glass. As if sensing my irritation, he raised his hand in defence, and began his story.

"Some of the things I am about to tell you may be a surprise, some may not," he started. *"Despite your father having betrayed my trust, I wish to emphasise that I mean you no harm. I have no doubt at all, that he would have kept many secrets from you and your mother, and almost certainly would have appeared to be a person of little consequence. In fact, your father was a highly skilled marksman during the Second World War, and afterwards worked in the Far East on important contract work."*

I felt my jaw drop. "No, no, no, no way. You have the wrong man. My father did go away a lot, but if you had really known him, George Worme was all talk and no action!" "I would politely ask, Miss Wilde, that you let me finish my story. Only then will you be able to grasp the truth." I shrugged, and relaxed back into my seat, allowing him to continue.

"During the Second World War, as a young man, my parents sent me to England to be educated. They arranged for me to stay until the Japanese had left Malaysia, and the War was over. Your father drank regularly at the Rifleman's Inn in Exmouth and at the same time did a profitable trade in black market goods. We students could obtain anything from your father; meat, chocolate, alcohol, cigarettes even guns if we had wanted them! He would also disappear, from time to time, on a friend's fishing boat, and return with money to burn. I found your father fascinating yet frightening. One night I followed him as he left the

Rifleman's Inn. He was very drunk, and with great difficulty made his way to the beach. For two hours, he slept in the sand, with his beret over his face, snoring loudly. Having got very stiff and cold, I decided that enough was enough, and started to climb out of my cramped hiding place between two sand dunes. Then all of a sudden, I became aware of the faint outline of a rowing boat, coming through the gloom towards the shore. I quickly went down on my knees and crawled out of sight. Your father sprang to his feet and lit his cigarette lighter. I was now crouched behind a damp wooden fence, which was covered in smelly seaweed, holding my breath. As I watched, two men climbed out of the boat and advanced towards your father. There were handshakes and much backslapping, but I could not make out their faces, until one of the men lit a cigarette. The light splayed briefly across a peaked officer's hat; a German officer's hat!"

The Prince's story was fascinating. He was obviously relating an actual experience from his student days, but sadly, I would have to tell him soon, that the man concerned was not my father. However, I remained patient as he took a long drink from his glass and continued.

"As you can imagine, I was horrified; a black market dealer was one thing, but a German collaborator was another thing entirely. The men sat huddled on the beach, deep in hushed conversation, for what seemed an age. Finally, all three walked to the boat, where your father was handed a long, thin bundle wrapped in sackcloth. Then the rowing boat, with the two men back on board, slowly and silently bobbed out into the gentle waves and disappeared back into the murky depth of the night."

"Your father set off immediately, hurrying along the beach in the direction of a slipway and onto the road. I removed my shoes, tied the laces together, and followed him in my stocking feet. His shadowy figure headed for the docks, around to the back of the yacht club and down wooden steps to a mooring. In the moonlight, the fishing boat rocked gently up and down in the swell, as your father disappeared below decks. Minutes later, he reappeared, without the bundle, and

quickly walked off towards town. I had to see what was in the bundle and ran as stealthily as possible to the wooden steps. The boat rocked sharply as I clambered aboard; the stench of fish and creosote was overwhelming. I listened carefully - not a sound - and climbed down into the single cabin below."

"I was in complete darkness and fumbled for my lighter. Apart from a couple of coiled ropes and crab pots, the cabin was almost bare. In the far wall was a tall locker and the door was only secured with a metal hook, so I carefully eased the door open and looked inside. Nothing, just some old oily rags and a couple of storm lamps. I splayed the lighter flame around the cabin; still nothing. Disappointed, I headed for the door and reached up for the handrail, which was loose and badly fitted. Suddenly inspired, I took the whole rail firmly in both hands and pulled. The rail and the board it was attached to came away in one piece, leaving a long thin cavity behind it. There was the package! My breathing suddenly sounded thunderous; suppose someone had heard me! I crept up to the top of the stairs and peeked out. Not a soul was in sight. I quickly returned and unwrapped the bundle. I had in my hands what appeared to be a very sophisticated rifle, along with some kind of telescope. The telescope seemed to fit on the top of the barrel; I had never seen anything like it before. I carefully rewrapped the parcel and returned it to its hiding place.

By the time I got back to the Rifleman's Inn, last orders had been called, and my friends were already heading for the car, singing at the top of their voices. Tommy, a Welshman and my closest friend, staggered over and flung his arms around me whilst chanting, "Down with the Japs, up with the Malays!" We piled into the old Morris and somehow found our way back to our lodgings in Exeter."

The Prince smiled and nodded as he recalled what was obviously a fond memory.

Chapter Three

The sun had sunk quite low in the sky, spreading a golden glow across the tree-tops. Long shadows lay across the lawn and a gentle breeze had begun to ruffle the blades of grass. Dippy had moved to the far side of the lawn to bathe in the last bit of sunshine and had relaxed enough to roll over onto his back in a most ungainly fashion. I realised that we had been sitting in one position for rather a long time, because the base of my spine was well and truly numbed. The Prince, meanwhile, had excused himself and, with the Gorilla's support, had made his way to the bathroom.

Despite the hour, I felt inspired to make a pot of Earl Grey tea. After all, this was an English country garden and I was entertaining a royal Prince! But how ridiculous; I had sat for the last couple of hours listening to an incredible story about my father related to me by a very small Far Eastern Prince. I scrubbed my fingernails at the kitchen sink and then reached for the cake tin. Fortunately, Sainsbury did a nice line in cream and jam sponges which easily passed for homemade. I placed my best white china, with the gold leaf rims, and the sliced cake onto a tray and stepped out into the still warm garden. The Prince had just returned to his seat and bowed politely as I placed the tray on the table.

"This is extremely kind of you, Miss Wilde, taking English tea has always been one of my favourite pastimes," he purred. I smiled and nodded. He may have thought, at this point, that I was warming to him, but in fact it was quite the reverse. My entire purpose was to keep the atmosphere as relaxed as possible to avoid bringing out the obvious evil side of this man's personality. In addition, I was keen to hear the whole story before I saw him and his Gorilla out of my sacred garden. "Please do continue, Your Highness, I'm keen to hear the rest of your story." I said rather too lightly.

"I hope that you are taking me seriously Miss Wilde, this is not just a 'story' but a very important piece of unwritten history," he hissed and his black eyes flashed with venomous intent. "I will not keep you too much longer, but I assure you, that once I have finished my story you will believe what I have told you and will also want to assist me in putting things right!" "I promise you, your highness, that I have no reason to doubt your story, but please understand that this is all proving quite a shock. The man I remember as my father was certainly a rogue, but a hired marksman, well, surely you can understand my incredulity," I said carefully. "Please do continue."

The Prince lit a small cigar, which looked large in his tiny bony hand, placed his free hand back on the table and continued. *"All the way back to our university lodgings, my mind was in turmoil. I resolved to discuss my dilemma with Tommy as soon as we were alone. Tommy, however, was much the worse for drink and fell asleep fully clothed as soon as his head hit the pillow. I sat on my bed, on the opposite side of the room, until the early signs of dawn began to seep through the curtains. Perhaps I should not involve my good friend, who had defended me so many times against the taunts of foolish locals, who assumed I was a 'bloody Jap.' I looked at Tommy, whose snoring was enough to wake the dead. His tousled black hair and carefully waxed moustache belied his underlying academic nature. Always good for a laugh and game for anything. But this time, I decided that I could not include him; the risks may be too great."*

"I had the following morning free and persuaded Tommy to lend me the Morris. I said that I wished to do a little sightseeing, and promised to be back for lunch. He was reluctant to let me go off alone, but I assured him that I would stay in the car to avoid hassle. I headed south down the Topsham road, leaving the cathedral city of Exeter behind me. I was soon motoring through open countryside and into the fishing village of Topsham. Another five miles, or so, and I would reach the Royal Marine camp, where I intended to speak to someone in a senior position.*

"There's a bloody Jap at the gate, claims to have an important message for

the Colonel!" The burly corporal bellowed down the telephone. "No, Sir, he's not in uniform, he's not armed, and he's alone. No, Sir, he's driving a Morris and claims to be a student from Exeter University!" "The Sergeant wants to know if you are surrendering or asking for asylum." The Corporal was now speaking to me. "Please tell your Sergeant, that I am a Malayan student and have some important information to impart, regarding a local man who is in collusion with a German officer!" The Corporal froze for a few seconds, and then as if suddenly awakened by gunfire, shouted down the telephone line to his poor sergeant. "The Jap says that he is a Malayan student and knows a German officer who is pretending to be a local! Yes Sir, right away, Sir!" The corporal blew his whistle and two equally burly marines rushed to attention. "The sergeant says that we are to impound the car and take the Jap to the guardhouse. A truck will collect him in five minutes!"

A flurry of activity, and I found myself quickly marched to the nearest Nissan hut. As you can imagine, I was already seriously regretting having presented myself to this elite force. Would they believe me or slap me in jail for the rest of the war? Poor Tommy, if I was not back for lunch he would be organising a search party, and almost certainly informing the police. Within minutes, I heard the sound of screeching brakes. The door burst open to reveal a large, red-faced sergeant and two even larger military policemen. I was beginning to feel smaller by the minute! With my feet dangling off the ground, I was then unceremoniously carried by my arms to the waiting truck. A speedy drive past yet more green and brown Nissan huts, finally brought us to a jerking halt outside another, slightly larger, almost identical building to the guardhouse. I was bundled out of the truck, through a cloud of dust and into a dark, musty room. The air was thick with tobacco smoke, and as my eyes became accustomed to the gloom, I became aware of three officers sitting behind a large green leather-topped writing desk. "My name is Colonel Barrett-Smyth," boomed the officer in the middle. "You have two minutes to convince us of your identity or we will immediately inform the war office that you have been placed in custody!"

As a precaution, I always carried my identification papers, which I promptly handed to the sergeant beside me. The sergeant, in turn, passed them to the Colonel and stepped back to attention. "So, you are a Malayan student and a royal Prince!" The Colonel looked disappointed. "Give the little man a chair and get some coffee in here!" he barked." I related my experience from the previous evening, expressing my concern that my friends should not know that I had been to the marines to report it. The colonel issued instructions to contact central command immediately. Coffee arrived, and the conversation turned to the problems in Malaysia and the colonel's own Far East experiences. Twenty minutes later the Sergeant returned, stood firmly to attention, and handed a signal to the Colonel. The Colonel read the signal carefully, leaned back in his chair and let out a low whistle. "We're instructed to inform you, you're Highness that central command is well aware of the activities of Mr George Worme and that things are already in hand. You are asked to return to the university and we are to thank you for your patriotism and concern over this matter." The colonel stood, saluted, and quickly left the room.

I drove back to Exeter in a state of bewilderment. It was as simple as that, thank you, but please go away and do not get involved was the message. "Where have you been?" shouted Tommy as he raced across the University car park, "You're already half an hour late for lunch. We'll be lucky if we get any vegetables let alone meat!"

Chapter Four

I turned on the shower and lifted my face up, letting the hot water spray hard and fast into my tense facial muscles. Slowly and firmly I massaged shampoo into my scalp until at last the tensions started to ease. The garden had been almost dark by the time the Prince had left. He was booked for two nights into the Bell Inn at Bickleigh and would be returning tomorrow for lunch. The last part of his story had knocked me for six. There was no question at all that he was talking about my father, as the photograph, defiantly thrust in front of me on the garden table, had left me in no doubt. After his visit to the Royal Marine camp, the young Prince had decided against imparting his secret to Tommy, or to take things further on his own account. He had, however, resolved to make himself popular with my father, by regularly buying him drinks and taking an active interest in his many 'tall' stories. The locals laughed at my father's stories of heroism, believing him to be just a local drunk. The Prince, however, listened very carefully, particularly when my father had been the worst for drink and might let slip some vital information. One day, to his amazement, he was to discover that the drunken image was just an act! The Prince had gone to the outside lavatory and come face to face with two local fishermen. They started to push him around, calling him a Jap bastard, amongst other things. My father had burst in, and in seconds had both men semi-conscious with their heads down the toilets, they had not even seen him coming! My father had looked the Prince straight in the face and warned him never to go anywhere unescorted again - at that moment he was as sober as a Judge!

When the war ended, and the Prince had completed his university education, he returned to Singapore. His father was about to take up a senior post in Kuala Lumpur. The family moved there in 1947 and the young Prince joined the Army as an officer and interpreter. In 1948, his father had played an important role in the re-organisation of Malaya. Lengthy negotiations were undertaken with local rulers and finally the new Federation was formed. The Federation was made up of eleven states that, whilst still under British protection and subject to their advice, had their own rulers. The Prince quickly established himself within, what was to him, a new and exciting country; taking every opportunity to move in the most affluent and influential circles.

The day before the Prince had left England, he and his student friends had paid a last visit to the Rifleman's Inn. My father was found slumped in a corner, under the sign 'Old fishermen never die, they only smell that way.' This time he was genuinely very drunk. The young Prince, having desperately wanted to find out more about my father's activities, took two pints of cider to his table and sat down. My father had raised his head and with difficulty acknowledged the free drink. He was obviously letting himself go, being unwashed and unshaven. With the war having ended, he was much less in demand and regularly short of the "readies." The Prince confessed to having followed him to the beach and to having seen my father with the German officers.

"They were good times," my father had chuckled, his Devonshire accent rather more obvious than usual. "Plenty of readies for us double agents. Lots of eager maids, lots of slaps on the back, I was in demand you know - couldn't do anything wrong in them days...."

A double agent, yes that explained a lot. The rolls of banknotes and free drinks after a lengthy fishing trip and the easy access to black market goods. Then suddenly, my father had grabbed the young man's wrist and held it firmly. "I hear you're going back to Malaysia, little wog. There ain't no work for me here; maybe you need contract work doing, if you know what I mean!" He winked, attempted a half grin, and started shooting an imaginary rifle at a table of drinkers. The Prince's friends were, at this time, singing heartily at the bar with a couple of local Devon maids. It was an opportunity to snuck out and walk my father home. At that time, he was renting a room in a terraced house in Imperial Road, which was no distance at all for a drunk, supported by a determined young man. My father's room had been extremely sparse and in need of cleaning; empty bottles littered the floor next to the unmade bed and the place stank of cider and stale tobacco. During the next hour, my father lay on the bed and told the young Prince everything. His life as a double agent and the rich rewards. His skill as a marksmen, the number of important German military figures he had assassinated and his misery as his services were no longer in demand; his brilliant cover as a local drunk and his desperation to find work in a similar field. The crazy thing was I had grown up in the fifties, listening to the same stories of heroism, only to be told by my mother that my father lived in a dream world and had played no part in the war at all. How could he have done, he was born with a shrivelled left arm and been denied the chance to fight for his country! Thus the heavy drinking.

I stepped out of the shower, wrapped myself firmly with a large cream towel, and sat down on the bathroom stool. I reached for a smaller towel and slowly twirled my long auburn hair into a tight turban. The Prince's visit had not only disrupted my peaceful existence but was almost certainly going to change the course of the rest of my life. I walked down to the kitchen and poured myself a large glass of red wine. It was now quite dark, although the moon and stars provided enough light to see my way out to the pergola and the old garden seat. An owl hooted from the barn, and the soft sound of paws padded over the flagstones. Dippy curled up over my bare feet and quickly commenced his restful, gentle snoring. The full-bodied wine smoothly washed over my tongue and down my throat. I relaxed.

I leant my head against an upright timber and drifted back to my childhood. I must have been about six, when my maternal grandfather had installed an old green beach hut in the back garden. I was small enough to slide under the back of the hut, when playing hide and seek with my friends. One day I found a handgun, wrapped in sacking, and took it up to my room. It remained hidden under my pillow for several days until my father came in and tore the room to pieces. My mother had warned me never to touch anything that did not belong to me, otherwise my father would be very angry. I never went under the beach hut after that.

Throughout my childhood, and early teens, my father's cruelty and drunken abuse of my mother, made both our lives a misery. But then, there were also days when he would bring us presents and we would dance together to the sound of the old wireless. However, my teens were shattered when, one cold and frosty night, my mother fell through my bedroom door suffering from a severe asthma attack. This was shortly after she had finally managed to persuade the courts to grant a separation order, forcing my father to leave the house. In my bare feet, I ran half mile to the nearest telephone box and rang the doctor; when I returned, my mother died in my arms. I was just sixteen.

My father begged to be allowed back into the house and promised to make things up to me. He had got some work which would take him away for a while, but when he returned he would buy me the prettiest clothes I had ever seen. I was afraid of my father, but felt strangely sorry for him at the same time. He stood on the doorstep in his black, leather trimmed beret and soaking wet double-breasted raincoat, clutching a leather carrier bag containing his few possessions. I stupidly agreed and let him stay; *'blood is thicker than water'* he used to say. Over the next two years, he was away a lot; when he returned he had money to burn and did buy me the pretty clothes he promised. He spent the rest of his time getting very drunk, in whichever pub had not recently thrown him out. Frequently, a policeman would arrive supporting a dishevelled figure, having found him collapsed in a gutter somewhere.

At eighteen, I left home and found myself a small property to rent. I had secured a full time job, with the local bookmakers, and was at last earning enough money to pay my own way. A girl I worked with moved in with me, which halved the rent and made life a lot easier. When we decided to have a house warming party I realised that I had no real friends, as I had always been afraid to take anyone home to meet my father. Sheila, my flatmate was partially deaf and had invited everyone from the deaf and dumb club. In addition, she had invited a Royal Marine whom she had met on the train on the way to work! That night the party went with a real swing. The music was extremely loud, due to the hard of hearing, and I enjoyed myself enormously. Just after ten thirty, the door burst open, and three large marines strode in. The blond one took my hand and kissed it, then he kissed my forearm, upper arm, and shoulder! When we danced, he threw me around the dance floor as if rock' n' roll was still in fashion. The following morning I woke up with a sore head and a grinning blond marine stretched out beside me!

I had vowed never to associate with the marines. Their camp was just a few miles out of town and those cocky, oversexed males were a damn nuisance. The local dance hall not only hosted live bands, but also regular fights between the locals and the marines. Dominic, however, was very different. He was not one of the lads, had ambition outside of service life and was, unfortunately for me, absolutely gorgeous. His sex drive was insatiable and I found myself hardly ever out of bed! Dominic was just twenty-one and had joined the Marines at the age of sixteen. He was bright, clever and very entertaining. In the October, I became pregnant. I told Dominic over a beer and a pasty at the Globe Inn at Lympstone. I was nineteen, totally in love, but not ready for marriage. Sadly, Dominic was due to leave for Singapore and would not be back for two years. I bravely declared that we should go our separate ways and that I would be perfectly all right on my own. He promised to write and after he left, I cried myself to sleep every night for the next two weeks.

Once the baby started to show, I decided to tell my father. He became strangely protective and insisted that I return home until after the baby was born. When Emma was born, my father showered me with gifts and promised he would stop drinking; he seemed to be trying to make up for his appalling past. I was determined to provide a good life for my beautiful daughter and having received no letters from Dominic, resigned myself to bringing her up alone. I organised a child minder and found myself a well-paid job in an Exeter stockbrokers. My career quickly took off and I was invited to go to London to take up a post in the City. I changed Emma's and my name to Wilde and we moved to the bright lights. Six months later I received a telephone call from Sheila; my *father was dead*.

Chapter 5

I awoke in bed to the sound of heavy breathing and the urgent licking of a very wet tongue. The sun was already pouring through the curtains and I was desperate for a wee. Stumbling into the bathroom I realised that it must be quite late, the beer, and wine of the previous evening had put me into a very long, deep sleep. I splashed a little cold water onto my face and staggered downstairs, my head was in need of a cold compress! I let Dippy out into the garden and plugged the kettle in. The kitchen clock registered ten fifteen, and the Prince would be arriving at midday!

Slowly, I pulled myself upstairs, clutching a cup of coffee and sat down on the bed. I had to get my thoughts together. I decided to put on a cool, cotton summer dress and selected a navy and white flowered version; pretty but not too informal. Sitting on the dressing table stool, I looked carefully at the reflection of the middle-aged lady and concluded that she was not looking too bad at all. The last couple of years had removed any excess fat, previously accumulated during endless desk-bound hours. Only one or two white hairs that easily blended into the mane of thick auburn hair surrounding the sun-tanned and freckled face. At one stage, I had been tempted to cut my hair, but the thought of seeing it lying on the floor felt like bereavement. Certainly a few more lines around the eyes, but my current lifestyle made up for these with a healthy outdoor glow. Back in the kitchen, I prepared a home-made vegetarian quiche and salad. The last of the home-grown strawberries were placed in a crystal dish and sprinkled with fresh mint and a little sugar. Then, I felt a wave of anxiety and reached for a wine glass; I had to allow myself half an hour to relax before the Prince arrived.

"You look quite delightful Miss Wilde," purred the Prince. "May I congratulate you on your choice of outfit? My late wife loved western clothes and in particular the pretty silks and satin fabrics available in Singapore. She designed her own dresses in the European style and wore beautiful hats like a mannequin. Her father was English, you know, I was the envy of my fellow officers when she agreed to marry me."

I had difficulty in imagining the Prince married, however, I smiled and made some comment about how lucky she was to have had such a proud and devoted husband. "You never married, Miss Wilde. Perhaps you were not so lucky in love?" "I fell in love once" I found myself saying, "but I was very young and a little foolish. He is rarely out of my thoughts despite the passing of twenty-five years. I have had relationships since then of course, but I was always looking for someone to replace him. Who knows...one day." "Your daughter, you brought her up alone. You have nevertheless proved yourself to be a strong woman, perhaps too strong and successful for most men to cope with!" He said genuinely.

I realised that the little man was getting rather too personal and was disturbed by his knowledge of Emma. I poured two glasses of sparkling, dry white wine and encouraged him to complete the story he had started the previous evening.

"By the early 1950's the Republic of Malaya was suffering much unrest amongst the various sultans" he began. "I decided to create an elite force of fighting men for the purpose of quietly disposing of the most troublesome of these rulers. I needed to find a marksman who could be bought in openly and without arousing any suspicion. 'Major George Worme, ex war hero and old friend from England' fitted the bill perfectly. A good disguise, don't you think? I flew to England and found him married with a baby on the way.

His wife, your mother, was a beautiful young woman and extremely sweet, but your father treated her badly. This was the first time that I had seen the evil side of his nature. Not surprisingly, he jumped at the chance to come back to Malaya with me and we embarked on creating his false identity, complete with officer's uniform and war record. As with all contracts carried out by your father, your mother had no idea what he was up to. Nobody, not even my own father was aware of Major Worme's real reason for coming to stay with me. I introduced *him to the expatriate society, which he took to with great relish. Bored wives were a particular attraction to him. At night, we carefully prepared for the first assassination, which was to take place one month after your father had arrived. The climate is always hot and sticky in Malaysia, and your father needed time to acclimatise and to familiarise himself with the terrain. Our journey would take us by train from Kuala Lumpur to Perai and then into the jungle on foot. We were to meet with my elite soldiers, before heading into the mountains where our quarry was taking a summer vacation. On the night of the assassination your father hopped around as if he was on hot coals; he could not wait to 'hit the little bastard right between the eyes!' His words not mine. As the light faded, we closed in on the camp, which was nestled in a clearing at the foot of a rocky overhang. The following information may, I am afraid, be rather shocking but it is important for you to understand the full extent of your father's wickedness. The Sultan sat surrounded by attentive servants and was being entertained by two half-naked dancing girls. As we watched from our hiding place, the Sultan rose up from his seat and dramatically exposed himself. The music grew more intense as the girls writhed on their bellies and slowly inched towards him. The Sultan began to gyrate his pelvis as each girl reached for one of his thighs. As your father raised the rifle to his shoulder, he started to laugh. When the shot rang out, the shock on the Sultans face was something to behold, he died with a bullet between his eyes and a full erection between his legs! Your father's laughter rang out through the jungle, echoing into the night, as we quickly made our way back down to the coast. When we returned to Kuala Lumpur he celebrated by sleeping with my married sister!"*

I had been so traumatised by the Princes description of the assassination that I had completely forgotten the lunch! As if recognising my need to recover, he apologised for having been rather too graphic and offered to pour me another glass of wine. It was, however, quite obvious that he had enjoyed shocking me despite his show of concern!

"My dear," he said consolingly, "I believe I can smell something delicious in the kitchen. Whilst you are fetching the lunch I will stretch my legs a little and go and admire the rhododendrons of which you have many varieties!" As if by magic, the Gorilla appeared at his side and helped him to his feet. Leaning heavily on his stick he set off in the direction of the ha-ha. Meanwhile, still reeling, I busied myself taking plates and salads out to the garden table. What I was learning about my father I could never have imagined in a million years.

At last, the Prince took his last mouthful of quiche and wiped his mouth carefully with his napkin. Dippy had decided that this visitor was not all bad, having received a large crust of bread from the hand of the little Malayan and sat gazing intently towards the now empty plate.

"In 1969 your father returned to Kuala Lumpur to complete one last contract," he continued. *"By this time he had many friends and many enemies in the area. Before he left Malaysia, he told me that he would be taking a short holiday with a lady friend. When I returned home I found a letter from my wife, to say that she was leaving with George and would be seeking a divorce."*

Despite the passing of many years, the distress still showed on the old man's face. He pulled out a silver cigar box, selected a ready cut cigar and lit it with a shaking hand. He handed the box across the table and pointed to the well-worn inscription. It read 'To Little Wog from George, forever best mates.' "Until that day I actually believed him" he said sadly. "My wife also took with her a valuable heirloom. It was a diamond and ruby studded necklace; an heirloom from my great grandmother. Your father knew it existed and I am certain that he would have persuaded her to hand it over. When your Father died you were his only known beneficiary, therefore you must have the necklace or have some evidence of its whereabouts!"

Once again, I felt my jaw drop. When I returned to Exmouth to arrange my father's funeral, the house was as empty of his belongings as it had always been. Certainly no evidence of a diamond and ruby necklace. Within three months, the house and furniture had been sold leaving me effectively rootless; however, some strange whim told me to keep the old leather carrier bag he always carried. It contained a toothbrush, a tin of Old Holborn tobacco and Rizla cigarette papers, a notebook (the last entry made recorded Emma's date of birth and above it an earlier date with an exclamation mark), a multi-purpose penknife and his battered beret. In the top draw of his desk was a brown package with my name on it which, when unwrapped, revealed a lovely gold charm bracelet. The note read; *'Dear Joanna, if you are reading this, my lovely, then I'm surely pushing up the daisies. The enclosed bracelet belonged to my mother, your grandmother. I would like you to have it and to maybe try and remember me with some fondness when you wear it. I know that I was never a good husband or father, but I did love you both, I just showed it all wrong. Also, I don't regret what I did after Emma was born because I believed it was in your best interest, I hope that you will one day understand.*

Your Dad.'

The last sentence had a strange ring to it. I could never fathom out its meaning.

Chapter 6

I placed the old leather carrier bag on the garden table. "When my father died, I went through the house with a fine tooth comb. He left nothing of value, other than this charm bracelet, which belonged to his mother. The carrier bag contains the only remaining memories I have; you are welcome to look through it, but I think you will find it a waste of time."

The note-book did prove to be of interest to the Prince. As he slowly thumbed through it he would occasionally nod and tut tut. "The last but one date was the day my wife died" he said suddenly. "I received an anonymous telegram to say that she had died of acute kidney failure. When the coffin arrived from Singapore, I removed the lid and gazed down at her ashen face. She was still beautiful, even in death and just thirty-five years of age. We gave her a full state burial, as she was loved and mourned by many people."

"I'm so sorry" I gasped. "It seems that my father destroyed more than one family during his short life, I only wish I could do something to help you." "You have already done a great deal, Miss Wilde," he said warmly. "You have welcomed me into your beautiful garden and allowed an old man to tell you his life story. To be quite frank, I did not really expect to find any trace of the necklace." He sat quietly for a few moments and sipped his wine. Then as if feeling the need to change the subject he embarked on a lengthy account of his military and political career, most of which seemed highly romanticised. Finally, he gave me a well-thumbed picture of the necklace and a copy of a Lloyds Insurance certificate showing that he was the rightful owner. He asked that if I should come across any information during the next seven days, to contact him at the Cadogan Hotel in Knightsbridge. He also handed me the photograph of my father, taken in a jungle clearing, as he no longer had need of it. We shook hands warmly and both bowed before he shakily climbed back into the stretch limousine. He rolled down the window and his lipless mouth stretched into an eerie smile. "Come and visit me in Kuala Lumpur; but make it soon as my physician does not hold out must hope for me. And, by the way, you look a lot like your mother. She was also very pretty with blue eyes and freckles, although unlike you, she was a natural blond. She would have been very proud of you. Goodbye Joanna"

I almost felt sorry to see him go; a strange sense of loss had come over me. For some time after the car had pulled out of the top of the lane, I remained standing at the gate. The events of the last two days had had a profound effect on me. Finally, it was a warm wet tongue on my bare ankle that brought me back to reality, then Dippy and I went to sit in the long grass at the top of Visitors Hill.

It was mid-afternoon and a perfect sunny day in early July. The long grasses swayed in the gentle breeze competing with the butterflies and bees for attention. Dippy sat bolt upright, with his warm body snuggled as close to me as he could get. He too gazed across the valley to the distant hills beyond, the patchwork of brown, yellow and green fields never failing to bring immense pleasure. "What are we going to do, Dippy boy?" I said aloud. "How can we simply ignore the events of the last two days? I suppose the first thing I must do is to record the whole thing on computer. If nothing else, it could be the start of an excellent novel!"

Dippy licked my chin sensing a certain amount of excitement in my voice. We stood up and commenced a slow walk through the woods down to the lake. I had inherited a number of mature rhododendrons that grew in abundance in the woods. Today, however, my mind was far too active to do my normal shrub gazing. Dippy had meandered on ahead, and my thoughts went back to the photograph left lying on the garden table. My father stood in the middle of a group of Chinese and Malayan soldiers. He was holding a rifle above his head and was making the victory sign with his left hand. I stopped, suddenly realising what I had seen. My father's left arm had been paralysed, yet in the photograph he was clearly holding his arm up making the victory sign! I called to Dippy and walked briskly back through the woods, over the hill and down to the house. The photograph lay where I had left it and sure enough, my father's left arm was raised up, doing a Winston Churchill, without any trouble at all!

Damn! I had to do some shopping as I had not replaced the last of the bottled beers. Instead, I poured myself a large gin and tonic and headed for the study. By the time, I had finished recording the Prince's story on the computer, I was feeling extremely tired and ready for an early night. I fell asleep under my feather quilt and dreamt the most amazing dreams. Come the morning I had made a momentous decision. I was going to visit Singapore and Malaya and attempt to track down my father's movements, during the last few years before his death!

"I would like to speak to Kong Beng Lim please." The Chinese telephonist had little English and passed me to a colleague. "Who shall I say is calling?" asked the lady who could speak English. "Miss Joanna Wilde from England," I said slowly. A few long seconds passed and suddenly Jimmy was gushing down the phone. "Joanna, we've missed you, are you back dealing again? When are you coming back to Hong Kong?" Lim, known as Jimmy, was probably the nicest Chinaman I had ever had dealings with during my international fund management years. Emma and I had stayed with his family during my fact finding company visits to Hong Kong. "Slow down Jimmy, give me a chance to answer one question at a time" I laughed. "No, I'm not dealing again and no, I'm not coming to Hong Kong in the near future. However, I am flying out to Singapore and I need your help to find a reliable and knowledgeable guide for both Singapore and Malaya. I want to do some extensive research in the area." "I'll speak to my cousin who knows everyone in Singapore" said Jimmy excitedly. "Diane and I will fly out to meet you, we've intended calling on my cousin and my brother for some time now. When do you intend coming?" "I have to make arrangements this end first, but I would hope to come over in two to three weeks' time." I replied, suddenly realising that I was actually committing myself to making this trip.

After putting the phone down on the enthusiastic Jimmy, I realised that I was probably rushing into this adventure of mine without any proper planning. I rang Emma. "Mum, how are you? Harry's just landed himself a superb job running the John Nichols Golf and Country Club. That means we have free access to all the facilities and it's the best club in the country now! Did you know that annual membership is £15,000 a year and you need to be sponsored by an existing member? Harry won't have to pay his fee anymore, instead they're going to be paying him - isn't that just amazing? Oh god! Finny has just come in with the dead rabbit the cat was playing with, hold on a minute!" The receiver clattered onto the table, and I listened to Emma shouting at Finny the lurcher and trying to retrieve the poor dead rabbit. "Blast" Emma gasped. "He's gone under the bed with it, can you believe it? Harry will have to sort it out, Finny doesn't take a blind bit of notice of me! Now where were we - oh yes, and my friends are so jealous. We thought we might have our wedding reception there, what do you think?"

"I didn't know you were getting married!" I gasped. "Of course you know, Mum, It's living in the depth of beyond that makes you to lose your memory all the time." Emma quipped. "Emma, I need your help. I want to fly out to Singapore to do some research, and need to be away for two to three weeks. I wondered if yourself, Harry and Finny would like to come down and house sit for me. It would be ideal for you all and you badly need to take a rest. Dippy would love to see Finny again and...." I was suddenly interrupted. "Actually mum, that's a brilliant idea, we have just been talking about taking one of those Landmark Trust properties for a couple of weeks; coming down to Devon would be an even better idea. Harry doesn't start his job until the middle of next month, leave it with me!" And she was gone.

Gosh, I had well and truly set the ball rolling. During stressful times, I would absentmindedly run my fingers over the charm bracelet, slowly turning it round and round my wrist. I found myself doing this now. I had worn the bracelet every day since I had found it, I suppose I considered it to be a sort of good luck charm and then started wearing it out of habit. Plump golden elephants followed each other on a never ending journey, linked to tiny golden bells to ring them on their way. Each elephant had a letter ornately carved on its side and I had given them names accordingly. Jumbo, Mimi, Oscar, Adam, George (after my father) and Monique (after my mother). There was nothing more I could do at that moment, so I decided to drive down to the Fisherman's Cot for lunch. Dippy and I enjoyed a salad sitting outside, overlooking the river and the waterfall. But it was difficult to relax, so we bought some beers and returned home to the pergola, the old bench and the timeless garden.

Chapter 7

The next two weeks proved to be amazingly busy. My wardrobe was now most unsuitable for the humidity of the Far East. Several trips to Exeter finally resulted in my purchasing enough cotton and linen clothes. I also selected a couple of quite sexy evening dresses, to grace my trimmer figure. Jimmy, and his lovely wife Diane, would almost certainly be arranging some evening socials in my honour, and I had every intention of making the best possible entrance. Emma and Harry would be arriving on the Saturday and had managed to arrange to stay for three weeks. Stocking up with dog and cat food, wine and beers was the last thing I had to do and a flying trip to the supermarket on the Friday at last completed my long list of 'do's'.

Saturday, late morning, and Dippy was barking and hyperventilating at the same time! The excitement of seeing the red Jeep arrive had sent him into a complete frenzy. Emma unzipped the back of the soft top and a flying grey lurcher hurtled through the air. Finny jumped the gate, clearing it by a good three feet, over a five foot high shrub and straight into my arms. The force of his rapid arrival sent me flying backwards onto the garden seat. The frenzied licking at last ended and it was Dippy's turn. The boys were so pleased to see each other that the thunderous running, leaping and circling went on for a full five minutes! "Well" gushed Emma, "who would have thought that I would be seeing you again so soon after your birthday! The traffic has been terrible, the motorway's full of Grockles - nose to tail, it's obvious they don't normally drive on the motorway - they haven't got a clue! You look pretty, I haven't seen that dress before is it new? Harry slept most of the way down; got a bloody hangover - he's only away from his rugby friends for three weeks, you would think it was three years!"

"Emma!" I said as loudly as possible without actually shouting. "Give me that suitcase. The kettle has just boiled, do you want tea or something stronger?"

"I expect Harry would like a beer but I'm detoxing. Would you prefer beer or tea, Mum says?" She was now talking to Harry, who smiled broadly flashing his white teeth that stood out like beacons against his deep suntan. "Look at his disgusting suntan" Emma whined. "He's spent the last two weeks on the golf course whilst I've been slaving away in the city."

I smiled at the pair of them. They absolutely adored each other and Emma's apparent moaning was purely her way of showing Harry off. They made a very attractive couple, both slim and small but with large personalities. Emma had dark auburn hair like mine and deep blue eyes like her father. Despite her moaning about Harry's tan, she was herself sporting a healthy brown glow. Harry was physically very fit, with dark brown hair and twinkling green eyes - Emma had always had good taste. "I did actually clean the house last weekend," I found myself saying, as I placed the tray of beers on the garden table. "Unfortunately, we had heavy rain on Wednesday and Dippy took what seems like half the mud from the garden across the sitting room carpet. It's still a bit grubby......" Emma raised her hand to quieten me. "For goodness sake Mum, please stop going on about cleaning that's the last thing we're concerned about. We're just relieved to be on our own for three lovely weeks without the damn phone ringing!" "Have you made a list of jobs you want doing whilst we're here?" Harry had joined us. "You may as well make the most of having a strong athletic man around the house." He pushed out his chest and flexed his right arm muscle. "For God's sake Harry, stop embarrassing me in front of my Mother!" Emma groaned. "Yes do leave us a list, well, one or two things maybe." "Don't worry darling, I haven't made a list" I smiled knowingly. "Harry is welcome to have a go at any outside repairs he might come across. But for the moment, let's relax and enjoy the sunshine. I've prepared jacket potatoes and salad for lunch."

It was so nice to be in their young and happy company. The rush of the last two weeks now seemed a million miles away. The fact that I was flying out to Singapore on Monday did not yet seem a reality, however, it soon would be. All the arrangements had been made over the phone, using old contacts and charge card. I would be staying with Jimmy's brother who had a wife, Julie, and three teenage children. In reality, I would have preferred to have stayed at Raffles Hotel, but I could not possibly let Jimmy down. His brother did, however, have a villa on the wealthy side of the island and I was assured that I would not want for anything. Jimmy and Diane would be at the airport to meet me and I was to liaise with my guide the following day. The guide was to be a European, who had married a Malayan girl. He was a Far Eastern historian and a part time trader in any number of things. He was the most knowledgeable man in the area, according to Jimmy's cousin, and had spent the best part of his life living near Kuala Lumpur. He did not come cheap, however, at $350 a day plus expenses, he had better be good.

On the Sunday night, we went out to dinner at the Bell Inn in Thorverton, and then walked over to the Exeter Inn for real ale. Many familiar faces sat around the bar and a certain amount of excitement seemed to be generated by the news of my departure to the Far East. Deep in my stomach, despite the third glass of ale, I could feel a long forgotten twinge of anxiety. The bar buzzed with laughter and good wishes, but I was rapidly becoming very apprehensive. Two years ago, I had buried myself in the peaceful undulating hills and now I was about to leave it all in search of my father's final years! "Don't forget to send us a postcard." John, the landlord's smiling face was just across the bar. "The chaps here want to know if one of them can come with you to carry your bags, if you know what I mean!" he said with a wink. "Excuse me. My mother is over forty, you know" said Emma sharply. "She's way past that sort of thing." "What, past carrying bags or getting laid?" Barked a very drunken fat Paddy from the end of the bar. "Fat middle aged drunken Irishmen definitely come into that category," snapped Emma, always on the defensive, "and I'm not talking about carrying bags!" Everyone was now looking at Paddy, waiting for his response. Then, as if by way of salvation, the doors flew open and the Exeter Morris men bounced in. "I think it's time to leave," said Harry, raising his eyebrows in disgust. "Come on girls, Joanna needs an early night. I'll ring for a taxi."

I have little memory of the journey home, but I do remember Emma putting me to bed and turning out the light. I fell into a very disturbed sleep and dreamt of Chinese soldiers running through jungle and a sweating fat Paddy carrying two suitcases and a large rucksack on his back. I seemed to have missed Jimmy and Diane, and was heading who knows where, into the jungle. Suddenly, a large hairy creature jumped on me out of a tree and then another grabbed at me from behind. I screamed and sat bolt upright much to the surprise of Dippy and Finny, who had just climbed onto the bed, expecting to settle down for the rest of the night. I looked at the clock, which read five forty five. I lay awake for some time and watched the sun slowly rise sending warm shafts of light through the slit in the curtains. I felt almost unable to move. My mind told me to get up, shower and to take the boys for a nice early walk. However, my body did not seem to be getting the message! I lay struggling against mind over matter until the alarm went at 6.30. What lay ahead of me was pure adventure; a fascinating journey into the past. I should have been ready to leap out of bed and embrace the day, but all I could feel was nervous tension. I heard the tap going in the kitchen and the kettle being plugged in. Finny leapt off the bed and hurtled down the stairs. Dippy climbed down a little more sedately and followed him. "Are you awake Mum?" Emma called, "Harry's taking the boys for a walk so you can get straight in the shower whilst I cook breakfast."

At last, I felt ready to start the day. I stretched, opened the curtains and I looked out over rolling hills to an exciting if mysterious, new horizon.

Chapter 8

Emma had insisted on driving me to the station. I can honestly say that I would have been most disappointed if she hadn't, particularly as I was embarking on a journey which to some extent could be a little dangerous. She had fussed over me like a mother hen, checking my bag for passport, writing materials, paracetamol, malaria tablets, insect repellent creams, tape recorder and charge cards although not necessarily in that particular order. "Now you promise to ring me as soon as you get to Jimmy's brothers. Don't fall in love with any stray dogs and above all, don't trust anyone with slitty eyes!" Emma said forcibly. Her lovely face looked up at me from the platform, with just a hint of a tear in her eye, she was genuinely concerned for my safety. "Emma, darling" I said consolingly, "you know that I plan everything meticulously and am no stranger to travelling alone. I intend having a bloody good time apart from coming back armed with all the research I need. You just relax and enjoy the countryside, you deserve a break and I'll get enormous pleasure knowing that I have been able to give you that opportunity."

Then suddenly, the train gave a gentle lurch and began to move slowly forwards. "Goodbye Mum, I love you!" Emma called through cupped hands. "Goodbye, darling. I love you too!" I cried and the small lump in my throat suddenly felt like a rock. The train curved away out of the station and Emma was gone. I turned back to my first class seat, sat down, took a very deep breath and reached for my travel bag. I spent the next hour recording the events of the two weeks leading up to my departure.

I hadn't told anyone, including Emma and Harry, about the Prince's visit. I didn't want to worry them unnecessarily and in any case, they would have the whole story once my research was completed. Around half past twelve, I headed for the restaurant car and indulged myself with a gin and tonic. It was quite strange being back amongst the dark suited businessmen again, watching the juggling of knife, fork, chunky mobile phone and filo-fax all at the same time. Two years of early retirement had mentally slowed me down and I found myself idly smiling in a wonderful mist of detachment. The prospect of the next three weeks research now filled me with excitement. Discovering that my father had led such an amazing double life, had somehow managed to lay a ghost, which had haunted me since the day he had died. It was, as a direct result of my childhood, that I had pushed myself to the limits of mental endurance in my career, needing to prove to myself that I could not only survive but survive better than most. My miserable childhood could now be put into context - the man had obviously been a psychopath. After my discovery, that my father's left arm had not been paralysed, I had telephoned the Prince at the Cadogan Hotel. He had explained that my father had been born with a deformed arm but paralysed, no. In Singapore and Malaya, he had acted the part of the wounded hero! It seemed to have had no effect on his ability to bed a large number of women.

On my arrival at Heathrow, I was met with the news that my plane was delayed by an hour and a half. Determined to continue with my relaxed mood I repaired to the VIP lounge for another Gin and Tonic. I spent a while thumbing through the pages of Tattler, until I was interrupted by the very sexy sound of a French male accent. "Excuse me Mademoiselle, but is this seat taken?" I looked up and into a pair of warm deep brown eyes. He was probably in his mid-thirties, slim, clean shaven and extremely handsome. "No, it's not taken. Please do sit down." I smiled, noting the number of empty tables around us. "Forgive me, but I could not help notice your lack of wedding ring" he purred. "Surely a women as beautiful as you cannot be without an adoring husband!" "Well, this one is without an adoring husband and hopefully always will be!" I laughed. His extremely handsome face fell. "You are not one of these, how you say, thespians are you?" he whispered, "That would be such a terrible waste!" "You mean Lesbian" I corrected him. "No, certainly not, however, that does not mean that I am in the market to be chatted up by a complete stranger." "Then we must cease to be strangers immediately" he beamed. "My name is Laurent DuPont; you may have heard of me, I am a fashion designer. I am travelling to Singapore to meet with potential buyers for my latest collection and I would be delighted if I could buy you another drink."

I can't say that I had ever heard of him, but what the hell, he was handsome, entertaining and extremely flattering; how could I refuse. From that moment on he never left my side, persuaded the air hostess to move him next to me in first class and insisted on champagne. By the time we landed in Singapore, I had heard his whole life story and he had somehow managed to squeeze far more information out of me than I would ever have dreamed possible. There was no question at all of my not meeting him for dinner the following night. He was staying at Raffles Hotel and would arrange the best table in the restaurant for eight o'clock sharp. A car would collect me at seven thirty.

As we stepped out of the plane at Singapore airport, the heat hit us like the full blast of a jet engine and that not unpleasant smell of humidity filled my nostrils. Within seconds, the humidity was enough to bring the perspiration prickling onto the surface of the skin. Laurent held onto my elbow carefully steering me through the crowds and into the cool air conditioned VIP reception lounge. He refused to leave me until he had safely placed me in the hands of Jimmy and Diane, who came rushing across the floor to greet me. Introductions were made, and by way of a temporary farewell, Laurent kissed me gently, though fully on the mouth.

"You have known this Laurent long?" Diane asked, as Jimmy organised a porter to take my bags to a waiting taxi. "Not nearly long enough" I laughed, as we linked arms and waltzed off in the direction of the smiling Jimmy. As usual, Jimmy had done me proud. His brother's house sat nestled in a lush tropical garden overlooking the twinkling blue sea. The views were fabulous, the house itself was luxurious and thankfully, air conditioned. It was close to midday when we arrived and I was grateful for a long cool shower and a change of clothes.

Lunch was laid out beautifully on the veranda and long cool glasses of iced fruit juice were passed round. Jimmy's brother, known as Mickey, introduced me to his wife Julie and the three children. The children ranged from nineteen down to fourteen, and wore the latest western fashions. Julie, however, was dressed in an oriental silk shift and trousers with her tiny feet perched high on thick cork soled sandals. Lunch was most pleasant and Julie had cooked almost entirely to cater for my vegetarian diet. Having spent the last twenty four hours almost completely without sleep, I excused myself immediately after the desert and retired to my room. I awoke to find Julie tip-toeing into the room with iced tea. "You have slept for five hours, Joanna, and I am sure that you will want to prepare yourself for the guests who will be arriving at seven o'clock." She bowed politely and hurried out of the room as silently as she had entered it.

I looked at my watch. My god, six o'clock and I hadn't even telephoned Emma. "Thank god for that!" squealed my sleepy daughter. "For all I knew you might have ditched in the sea. Everything is fine here. I was surprised that you had organised the cleaning lady though, I told you not to worry about it. Mind you, she did a very thorough job, spent the whole day here! She said that you had already paid her; I hope that was right Mum. Where on earth did you find a Chinese cleaner in the middle of Devon? By the way, Dippy's got awful wind; I suppose its old age. Oh, Harry wants a word; I'll speak to you in a minute!" I sat down on the bed. My heart was racing and my body had frozen. "Hello, Joanna, hello!" I could faintly hear Harry's voice, but I was too shocked to speak. What Chinese cleaning lady, what the hell was going on? I gathered my thoughts and put two and two together. This must be something to do with the Prince; he had arranged to have the house searched! My god, Emma and Harry may be in danger; what the hell was I going to do? Over the last two weeks I had spent a lot of time on the phone making all my arrangements, he must have bugged the telephones, how else could he have known exactly when I would be going away? "Joanna, are you there?" Harry was shouting. "Yes Harry, I'm so sorry I dropped the phone, you wanted to speak to me." I managed to sound quite calm in the circumstances.

"Do you want the old fallen tree chopped up into logs? It would be a good workout." "Yes, yes please Harry; that would be great" I said briskly. "There is something else you could do for me. I'm going to be away for Emma's birthday. I would like you to take her out to lunch at Denleys today and put it on my bill. I've already booked a table for one o'clock. Then you can take her to that lovely soft furnishing shop just down the road, and buy a couple of those throws she was admiring." "Our favourite restaurant, sounds great, it will be a pleasure. Thanks Joanna." Harry said a few words to Emma and she was gushing down the phone. "You're spoiling me again Mum. I'm still annoyed with you for taking so long to ring though and you do realise that it's two o'clock in the morning here! I'll speak to you again in a few days, now you take care!" And she was gone.

What should have been a delightful evening proved to be quite a strain. I excused myself before midnight and snuck out for my bedroom. I carefully set the alarm for thirteen hundred UK time and climbed between the cool sheets. I sat bolt upright when the alarm went and hastily switched it off; hopefully nobody would have heard it. I looked up the number for Denleys Wine bar in my address book and dialled the number. The familiar sound of Clive's voice floated over the noise of faint laughter and the clink of glasses. "Hello Clive, its Joanna" I said in a low voice, "can you hear me all right?" "Loud and clear" was the singing reply. "By the way, you forgot to book the table, but I fitted them in anyway." "Clive, I need to talk to Harry without Emma knowing it's me. Can you use your usual way with words and get him to the phone?" "Leave it to me" he sang, "no sooner said than done."

"Joanna?" Harry said inquiringly, "more surprises for Emma no doubt!" "Harry, I want you to listen very carefully" I said urgently. "It's possible that you may both be in danger. I am sorry to have to spoil your lunch, but I could not explain over the phone at the farmhouse."

Harry listened in silence as I quickly gave him a summary of the Prince's visit, and my reasons for believing that the cleaner had been sent to search the house and the gorilla may have bugged the phones. He had been a good ten minutes in the loo. Harry felt convinced that they were probably not in danger, but would remove any bugs whilst Emma was occupied elsewhere. I knew I could trust Harry to take care of the situation; I felt hugely relieved. Harry took down my number and promised to report back with any news. It was now quite clear to me that I was, almost certainly, being followed here in Singapore. Feeling horribly vulnerable, I turned off the lamp, slipped back between the sheets and drifted into a very restless sleep.

Chapter 9

Breakfast was a cheerful affair with the children talking thirteen to the dozen. I was impressed with their English and commented on this to Jimmy whilst taking coffee on the veranda. "They're being educated at British run colleges" Jimmy explained. "Mickey is a very successful rubber exporter and all trade and commerce is conducted in English. Here in Singapore, it's considered impolite and foolish not to have an excellent command of the English language. His two sons will join him in the business although his daughter wants to be an air hostess. She's only fourteen mind, things might change!"

"Julie and I are going shopping today" said Diane as she joined us with her coffee. "Your guide will be arriving at ten o'clock, so you're not going to have much time to shop. Is there anything you need?" "I don't think so, thanks Diane. How much do you know about this guide? Julie says he's a bit of a hunk" she laughed teasingly. "Are you sure, you don't need a chaperon?" "Take no notice of Diane" laughed Jimmy. "We don't know very much, other than the fact that he has spent most of his adult life living in Singapore and Kuala Lumpur. He spent some time in the services and is an expert with guns. More importantly, he has published several history books on the area that are used by the university. He also has all the right contacts in high and, dare I say, low places. My cousin insists that he can be trusted as he has worked alongside him negotiating with the various Sultans for trade reasons. He is also fluent in English, Chinese, Malay and Tamil." "He sounds perfect" I enthused, "I can't wait to meet him!"

At 10 o'clock sharp, the doorbell rang. I made a quick dash to my room and changed into a comfortable cotton dress and flat sandals. A glance in the mirror resulted in the need for a hairbrush and hair-band. Then I rummaged in my shoulder bag and checked for note pad, pens, tape recorder and camera. Fat chance of an historian being a hunk, but nevertheless I checked again in the long mirror and put a touch of pink lipstick on. "Joanna, your guide is here!" called

Julie as she gently tapped the door. I opened it to find her grinning uncontrollably. "He really is quite dishy, Joanna, you may have difficulty in concentrating on your research!" She whispered. "Behave yourself, Julie, what would Mickey think of you!" I laughed. The tall, well-built figure stood staring out to sea on the veranda. I had to admit that at least from the rear, and in those shorts, he had a certain something. Jimmy rose from his seat as soon as I stepped through the door.

"Ah, Joanna, I would like you to meet your guide, Mr Dominic Francis. Mr Francis this is Joanna" he said enthusiastically. The blond head turned and Dominic's right hand was thrust forward in greeting. Without thinking, I placed my hand in his and we both froze in instant recognition. For several long seconds we stood staring at each other in disbelief, until he managed to find his voice. "My God, Joanna!" he gasped, "Is this some kind of cruel joke. What the hell is going on?" He snatched his hand away, as if it was on fire, and took two paces backwards. Angrily he spun round and turned on Jimmy. "I don't know what you're trying to pull here, but there is no way that I am working with that woman!" he shouted and stormed off in the direction of the front door, slamming it behind him. As the sound of the car engine roared off and faded into the distance, I reached for a chair and sat down in very slow motion. "Joanna, I can't imagine what was wrong with the man!" Jimmy was saying. "Quickly Diane, get her a brandy I think she is close to fainting!" Close to fainting, I should say so; I had just come face to face with Emma's father! His face was still so vivid, the blond hair, the deep blue eyes, the eyebrows bleached white by the sun and the deep golden tan. I could still feel his hand in mine, but the anger in his voice....I had started to shake. Diane was thrusting a glass into my hand and was trying to get me to drink; the brandy hit the back of my throat and burned into my chest. "I'm so-so sorry" I stammered "but I've just had the most awful shock. I think you should both sit down." They drew up chairs and sat either side of me each clasping one of my hands. "Dominic Francis is Emma's father" I said weakly. "I haven't seen him for twenty five years!"

"Great Scott!" shouted Jimmy, in his best upper crust English fashion. "This is the man that abandoned you to bring up your child alone and he has the nerve to speak to us like that!" He was furious. "I will track him down immediately and give him what for. I'll go and ring my cousin and find out where he lives!" "No, wait!" I called after the retreating little Chinaman to whom I owed so much. "No, Jimmy you must give me time to think. I will have another brandy and perhaps you should have one too."

Jimmy poured us all brandies and we sat in silence for a few minutes. My mind was fighting with the urge to rush after the man whose memory had prevented me from falling in love with anyone else. I remembered his laughing face as he ran down Shelly Beach to the sea, then accidentally diving into only four inches of water and his embarrassment as I gently bathed the scratches left by the gravel sea bed. I remembered the fun we had playing darts in Lympstone, and the way he carried me around like a baby when I was recovering from a dislocated knee. I remembered nothing but love, I could not relate to the new Dominic and the smouldering hate I had seen in his eyes.

I had regained a little of my strength and walked down the steps to the garden. Diane had insisted on coming with me, but I had wanted to be alone. The sun was very hot and I was glad of the straw hat that she had thrust into my hand. I felt a mixture of fear and longing both at the same time. I had to see Dominic again, at least to talk to him about Emma. How could he not want to know about his beautiful daughter, he must have wondered about her? I never had understood why he had not written, at least to say that he wanted to finish things. We were both so young; I had not expected him to come back after the Singapore posting and marry me simply because of a baby, but we had loved each other so much.... I sat for some time in the shade of a pergola watching the koi carp splash and tumble over the manmade waterfall. The garden was very beautiful and it eventually had quite a calming effect on me.

Suddenly, I had a desperate need to hear Emma's voice and to check that all was fine back in Devon. "Hi, Mum!" Gushed a cheerful Emma. "We had a lovely lunch and I've chosen two of those gorgeous blue and white striped throws for the sitting room. It was a lovely surprise but I thought that we were going to celebrate when you got back. You are getting me lots of other presents I hope. By the way, do you usually have problems with the boiler, it keeps firing and then going off; Harrys got it in pieces at the moment. We don't need the central heating but I do prefer to cook on the Stanley." "There's a telephone number pinned up on the kitchen notice board. Some chap in Tiverton, he'll sort it out." Good for Emma, she always managed to bring me down to earth. Harry also passed a message to say that all was fine 'in the garden' which obviously meant that all was fine generally.

The sound of a light tap on the door and Julie's little flat nosed, pretty face appeared. "I'm so sorry to hear about your upset" she said kindly "is there anything I can get you?" Almost immediately, the door-bell rang. "Joanna, Joanna!" Diane came rushing into the room almost completely hidden behind an enormous bunch of red roses. "These are for you, could they be from Dominic, perhaps he wants to apologise!" I carefully opened the small white envelope whilst the two Chinese faces craned to get a closer look. *"To my beautiful Joanna, your car will arrive at 7.30pm, your devoted slave Laurent XXX."* I had completely forgotten him. What with all the stress and excitement of the last twenty four hours, it was hardly surprising! "Oh, you must go, and wear something very sexy!" laughed Julie. "That will give this Dominic something to think about!"

But I did not want to give Dominic anything to think about, I just wanted to talk to him to tell him that I was not angry with him.....that I had never stopped loving him. But then Dominic was obviously not the slightest bit interested in seeing me, he had made that quite plain. I would go out this evening and enjoy Laurent's intoxicating company; I hadn't come all this way to be miserable. At seven thirty sharp, a white Rolls Royce pulled up outside the front door. I stood in front of the long mirror and looked at the woman in the low backed cerise silk dress and hummed my approval. I had left my long hair loose over my bare shoulders having clipped a gold slide into one side. I slipped into stiletto sandals and threw a black pashmina over my shoulders. Both Jimmy and Mickey whistled their approval as I crossed the entrance hall, whilst Diane and Julie clapped with delight. I sank into the car's leather upholstery and felt wonderful. On the way to Raffles, I counted over one hundred elephants on my charm bracelet as I slowly twisted it round and round my wrist.

Chapter 10

At 7.30 in the evening Singapore was very busy. Many buildings still reflected its colonial past, like the Victoria Memorial Hall with its imposing clock tower. City Hall came into view, with its magnificent white columns and rows of red, white yellow and blue flags. According to the driver, the offices of the Prime Minister were housed here. On the roads, American and Japanese cars rubbed shoulders with scooters and carriages attached to bicycles; I made a mental note to find out their local name. And so to Raffles Hotel and it's newly painted colonial facade. The hotel had been recently refurbished, turning it back to its 1930's grandeur. I swept out of the Rolls intending, to make the best possible impression and glided towards the entrance. The doors were opened as if by magic and, after much bowing by front of house, I was led into the lounge bar. "Joanna!" gushed an enthusiastic Laurent, "You look stunning, beautiful - there are no words to adequately describe the angel I see before me!" I laughed and remembered thinking, my God, how typically French. "Why Laurent, you might make this angel blush. But I must return the compliment; you look so handsome in your beautiful suit. It must be one of your own designs!" I had to admit the Frenchman could have turned any woman's head at that moment. He was about five foot eleven, slim and wore his clothes very well. His dark swarthy looks were quite captivating.

We ordered champagne and relaxed over a very exciting menu. Laurent wanted to order the most expensive dish, however, on realising that I did not eat meat or fish, he personally instructed the head chef to cook something exotic with vegetables and fit for a queen. His visit to Singapore had proved successful; he was arranging to bring his collection over to be modelled for the Prime Minister's Wife and all the other important women on the Island. I congratulated him and felt myself quite choked by his excitement; I was genuinely very pleased for him. "You will still be here during the first week in August, won't you?" He asked, reaching for my hand. "It will give me great pleasure if you could join me as my personal guest at the fashion show. I would be so proud to have the beautiful English writer, Joanna Wilde, at my side!" "I am not a writer yet, mind you, I will not be at all surprised if I return to England with some pretty good ideas for my long awaited a first novel."

Laurent was absolutely wonderful, it was impossible to feel anything but pleasure in his company. I was astonished and rather sad to find how quickly the coffee and Port had arrived; the time had just slipped away. A commotion in the doorway to the restaurant, suddenly took our attention away from each other. Two waiters were struggling to prevent someone from coming into the room. "Can you see what's happening?" I asked Laurent. My view was obstructed by a potted palm tree. "Some large man is arguing with the head waiter, it looks as if he is improperly dressed. He's just pushed one little Chinaman into the sweet trolley and he's heading this way!" Dominic came to an abrupt halt and stood glowering over the table. "I telephoned your friends' house to arrange our schedule for tomorrow. I was told that I would find you here, but I didn't expect to find you with some greasy Frenchman!" He stormed.

Laurent rose angrily to his feet. "How dare you speak to Joanna like that, you English pig!" Dominic grabbed the unfortunate Frenchman, who was at least four inches shorter, by his tie and pulled him across the table sending glasses and cutlery flying! "Now stop it this instant" I commanded. "You're acting like a couple of overgrown schoolboys! I would be grateful, Dominic, if you would apologise to Laurent and leave. I'll be ready at nine o'clock in the morning and we can discuss the schedule from there."

"Then I would suggest that you go home and get an early night. We'll have a busy day tomorrow." And with that last sarcastic comment, he turned on his heel and stormed out, leaving behind a lot of very relieved diners and waiters. Laurent had re-seated himself, but was looking very distressed. "I cannot allow you to associate with this man" he whispered, "I am afraid that you may come to some harm."

"Dear Laurent, you have no need to worry; I do know what I'm doing. Dominic is an old friend and is also the best possible man for the job." "I feel that you may have some other reason for seeing him tomorrow. Are you in love with him?" Laurent asked quietly. "Really, Laurent," I laughed weakly "of course not, you're just a big romantic. Now come on, the evening is still young and you did say something about dancing, so what are we waiting for?"

The rest of the evening was wonderful. Laurent and I danced until past midnight and finally collapsed exhausted onto a large comfortable sofa in the luxurious lounge. More champagne was ordered and we sat huddled deep in trivial conversation until gone one. Suddenly, I realised that staying any longer would mean only one thing. It would have been so easy to have gone to Laurent's room and to have spent the night in the arms of this delicious Frenchman. I murmured that I really should go as I had an early start the next day. Laurent took me in his arms and traced the outline of my lips with his fingertips. "Darling Joanna" he said softly, "I am afraid that if you leave now I will lose you forever. I have arranged for champagne and chocolates in my suite and the bed is too cold and large for one, especially a man in love." My feet tingled as he kissed me and his passion flowed like liquid honey. But it was Dominic that I was kissing; it was Dominic's hair between my fingers and Dominic's body pressed close to mine. I gently pushed Laurent away and, touching his cheek with my hand, I promised that we would meet again before he flew back to Paris.

The city had turned into a mass of swirling lights and crowds of late night revellers, as the Rolls swept silently through the streets and out into the suburbs. I laid my head back against the rich leather headrest and closed my eyes. For a few seconds I slipped into sleep and Dominic's domineering figure loomed out of the darkness, with the limp body of Laurent under his arm. The body was thrown across a dining table and Dominic took out a gigantic knife and fork..... "We have arrived, Miss Wilde!" The electronic voice of the Chinese driver came over the intercom. The door was being opened for me, and Jimmy was helping me up the steps and through the front door. "I'm sorry Jimmy" I said with difficulty "I must have fallen asleep." I remembered the sheet being gently placed over me, and mumbling something about Dominic and nine o'clock. I then fell into a very deep sleep.

The shower was a rather rude awakening. My head felt like nothing on earth, my tongue was swollen and it didn't seem to belong to me. It seemed best to do everything in slow motion and preferably sitting on the side of the bed and not moving, all at the same time.

"Joanna, you had better drink this and at least two large glasses of water. You're completely dehydrated and have an enormous hangover to boot!" Julie placed the tray on the bedside table. "You mumbled something about nine o'clock before you fell asleep; it's now eight thirty!"

I was enormously thirsty and drank the fruit mixture in one go. "Yes, Dominic arrived at Raffles last night and nearly caused a fight, he's collecting me in half an hour." "Then you had better let me dry your hair or you'll never be ready at this speed!" Whilst drying my hair Julie managed to get the whole story out of me, from the arrival at Raffles to the last passionate kiss goodbye. "I haven't met this Laurent yet," Julie smiled "but I would definitely choose him rather than that rude Dominic."

I looked in the long mirror. I had chosen the safari shirt and shorts and had tied my hair up into a loose knot. If I was going to be spending the day out then I wanted to be as cool as possible. Julie also lent me her straw hat, which could tie under the chin if needed. Dominic was bang on time, and coldly escorted me to the latest Limited Edition Wrangler Jeep. He had removed the rear and side windows leaving the canvas roof to deflect the hot sun. Up until he had strapped on his seat belt he had remained cold and silent. "Before we start out, I want to make one thing absolutely clear" he said firmly. "What happened between us in the past is dead history. I have no intention of discussing it and my only reason for being here is because we have a contract to work together. I have Susie to think about now and she is my only concern, she knows nothing about us and that is the way it will stay!"

"Well that just suits me fine" I said angrily. "I assume that you have also worked out today's schedule, which you don't intend discussing with me either." "Now you're being petty" he stormed. "If madam is agreeable I suggest that we spend today introducing her to Singapore." And with that statement, he engaged first gear and we set off at speed towards the Pan Island Expressway.

Chapter 11

Over the next two hours, Dominic described Singapore's origins and I learnt that it had been a port for several hundred years. We visited Sir Stamford Raffles statue, several important buildings and a noodle farm. I asked few questions and recorded everything Dominic told me on tape. He described, with some enthusiasm, Singapore's trading history which was and still is, the most important part of the island's economy. Tens of billions of dollars-worth of goods were being exported and imported each year. Dominic had a personal interest in company making machinery and metal parts. That particular industry constituted over 29% of the island's own production of products for export. By midday, I was feeling pretty exhausted and tentatively suggested a break for lunch. "We'll stop off and buy cooked prawns, noodles and vegetables." Dominic stated. "They're my mother-in-law's favourite and we'll go and have lunch with her." "Should you not ring her first?" I asked not just a little surprised. "Chor Ling lives in one of the few remaining kampongs on the island, that's village to you, and she doesn't have a phone. Most kampongs have been pulled down to make way for modern flats or factories and her own village is next on the list. It will be interesting for you to see the old way of life before it disappears completely."

We stopped at an open air market and Dominic purchased the ingredients for lunch. He spoke fluently, in what I later discovered was a Chinese language called Teochew. The market was quite close to the dominating tower blocks that housed many hundreds of families. Long poles of brightly coloured washing were strung out under almost every window. The gaps in between the blocks had meticulously mowed grass and neat rows of trees, giving the impression of ordered cleanliness. "Are the people happy living in these blocks?" I asked as we drove off and into a rather greener area, where pockets of the original jungle could be glimpsed. "Yes, the majority are happy. You have to remember that most people in the flats used to live in pretty primitive conditions, which Chor

Ling still has to suffer to some extent. She does have running water to her hut now, however, only two years ago she was still having to do her washing in the stream. She will miss the jungle and her plants, but she is actually looking forward to moving next week, now she's received her letter from the Government.

"You're very fond of Chor Ling, I think; do you manage to see her very often?" I asked, immediately regretting such a personal question. Dominic surprisingly did not seem to mind.

"Yes, she has been like a mother to me and in return I try to be a good son. She has suffered great losses over the years including her husband, a Malayan, a son and a daughter." Dominic then abruptly changed the conversation to the subject of our schedule over the next two weeks, and at this point, I explained that I needed to discuss with him the reason behind my visit to Malaysia. This would then determine our next course of action. The Jeep was proving its worth as the road became somewhat holed and muddy. The last day of heavy rain had been such a deluge that the monsoon drains were still quite full on each side of the road. Then we were driving into Chor Ling's village and brightly uniformed school children were running alongside the Jeep. A tiny grey haired lady sitting in a wicker chair rose to her feet and a broad, somewhat gappy grin, spread over her face. She wore a brown and white flowered shirt with matching trousers and her hair had been cut short and neatly set in small curls. Dominic jumped down from the Jeep and swept her up into his large arms. Seeing me watching she struggled free, adjusted her clothes and patted her hair. I climbed down and walked over to greet her, feeling a little humbled by the previous show of affection. She bowed deeply and I did the same, then taking my hands she let out a flood of words in Chinese. Dominic laughed. "Chor Ling says that she hopes her darling Susie knows that I am spending time with a beautiful English lady." He then went into rapid conversation with her following which she nodded smiled and took my hand. I was led into a small wooden house with a corrugated metal roof. Inside was a single room with a curtain hiding a bed in one corner. On the opposite wall hung three framed pictures that were obviously of her deceased husband and two children. A small decorated shelf had been placed underneath where she had lit sticks of incense and candles in their memory. The curling smoke wafted slowly up to the ceiling and across the room, filling my nostrils with its heavy intoxicating perfume. The food, we had purchased earlier, had been put in foil containers and was still quite warm. Dominic bought plates from a cupboard and Chor Ling produced small cups of soya bean milk. Surprisingly, she had a full size wooden table with four chairs by the door and we all sat down to enjoy the lunch. After eating, Chor Ling produced a photo album, which contained sepia photographs of her husband in military uniform and later on, black and white pictures of five children of various sizes. Dominic gently eased the album away from her before she had shown me everything, which caused rather a rush of questions from Chor Ling. Dominic put his hand on hers and spoke to her in Chinese, which calmed her down. "I have just explained that we cannot stay any longer because you're paying for my time" he said to me. "I really don't mind staying a little longer if Chor Ling would like us to." "No." Dominic was adamant "I will come back and see her with Susie in a few weeks' time."

Suddenly, I felt stupid waves of jealousy wash over me. He had everything, the wretched Susie, an adoring mother-in-law and a real feeling of belonging. He did not want me to encroach any further than this fleeting introduction. I stood and bowed deeply to Chor Ling and asked Dominic to thank her for her hospitality. She took my hand and suddenly spied the charm bracelet. "This is pretty," she said, in halting English and then asked Dominic a question. "Chor Ling says that she once saw a bracelet like yours many years ago, it was worn by a little white girl, although she can't remember where." He explained. I frowned. "It must have been something similar, this one belonged to my grandmother."

"I'm in need of a cold beer," Dominic announced as we drove back towards the concrete and tower blocks. "There's a good hotel bar near here with air conditioning. It will also give you a chance to freshen up."

I filled the wash basin with cold water and scooped handfuls up and over my face. Patting my face and neck dry, I looked myself in the mirror. The face was the same, but the woman had changed. I had found Dominic and at last, the cloud of not knowing had been lifted. But the man was a complete stranger and I was rapidly beginning to feel like an intruder. I returned to the lounge. Dominic was sat at the bar deep in conversation with a Chinese, who he obviously knew well. The man let out a loud laugh and turned to watch me walk across the room. As I reached the bar, he stepped forward, kissed my hand and motioned me towards the stool between himself and Dominic. "Max has bought you a beer; you do drink beer don't you?" Dominic asked. "Yes, thank you Max. I'm very fond of the occasional glass." I said defensively. "Spoken like a man," laughed Max and promptly slapped me across the bottom. My anger must have hit Max right between the eyes, as he apologised for his mistake before I had a chance to say anything. "Max, I would like to introduce Joanna Wilde." Dominic cut the atmosphere with a sharp knife. "I'm helping her with some research. Joanna, Max is Singapore's Chief of Police."

Max stood, bowed and offered to provide any information he could to assist me. I said it was quite likely that I would call on him over the next couple of weeks. I motioned to Dominic that we needed to have a discussion, and proposed that we moved to a table in the bay window. He ordered two more bottles of beer and we made ourselves comfortable. Over the next hour, I told him about the Prince's visit and my shock at discovering my father's double life. Dominic sat in silence absorbing these revelations. He had met and instantly disliked my father, the feeling had been mutual. Finally, he stood and gazed out the window. "It doesn't surprise me in the slightest!" He said, turning back towards me. "He was a nasty piece of work, I'm glad to hear that he's dead. So the task is to track down his movements during the last couple of years of his life, this is going to be an interesting one. Well, Joanna you have the right man for the job and I propose that we set out for Kuala Lumpur tomorrow. I will telephone Susie and ask her to make up a room for you."

Chapter 12

Dominic unlocked the door of the Jeep and held it open for me. For the first time he managed to look me straight in the eyes, as I passed just inches away from him and climbed into my seat. For a split second, I felt certain that he wanted to snap out of his formal, and at times, hostile mood. But the moment passed as he climbed into the driver's seat, set the Jeep in motion and off past the high rise flats and a huge public swimming pool full of splashing brown bodies. Before leaving the hotel, Dominic had explained his reasons for travelling to Kuala Lumpur the following day. At his home, he had all the research information needed to find evidence of my father's activities during those last few years. He had become quite excited at the prospect of filling in several gaps in history to include a number of unsolved assassinations. The Prince was well known to him as was his son, Hussein. In the late seventies Hussein had confessed to being a pro-Chinese Communist. Whilst a leading writer in the country he had engaged chiefly in spreading pro-Soviet and anti-American propaganda. I had emphasised my concern over the Prince's obvious determination to find the ruby and diamond necklace and that it was possible we were being watched. Dominic had laughed heartily and said that we could be absolutely certain of it! I also learnt that the Prince was known to be dying of Leukaemia and was not expected to survive more than a few weeks. This would explain why he had risked coming to see me and had effectively spilt the beans. Dominic dropped me back at Micky and Julie's house just as afternoon tea was being served on the veranda. Dominic declined to stay as he had a number of people to see and would collect me and my bags at nine o'clock in the morning. Julie and Diane were like school girls, desperate to hear about everything we had said and done. "But you can't go and stay at that Dominic's house," Julie gasped "what will his wife think?" "She doesn't know about us, and in any case, she has no reason to be concerned" I said firmly. "Dominic has all his research material there and Susie is making up a room for me." But I was concerned, in fact, I was terrified. My heart had missed a beat when Dominic had declared his intention to take me to his home. Susie was his wife and that was that, for God's sake, I could hardly have expected him to remain alone all his life. Nevertheless, I managed to relax over a very English tea. Jimmy joined us from the garden and enthused over the size of the rare tropical plants that Julie had nursed from seedlings. In many ways, I would be sad to leave in the morning, particularly as I had spent very little time with my delightful hosts. Jimmy and Diane would also be leaving in the morning for Hong Kong and it was agreed that we should all go out to eat that evening. As I finished my second cup of tea, the telephone rang and Julie scurried off to the sitting room. "Joanna!" she squealed "It's your lovely Frenchman with the very sexy voice!"

"Joanna, my darling English rose" purred Laurent. "I have not stopped thinking of you for one second since the moment you left. I must see you before I fly to London tomorrow, my heart will break if I cannot look into your beautiful blue eyes and feel your lips on mine again." Despite Laurent's obvious continental charm, a large lump still found its way into my throat and almost took my voice away. In different circumstances, I would have been straight into a taxi. "Oh, Laurent" I gushed wiltingly. "I'm so sorry, but I'm leaving for Kuala Lumpur first thing in the morning and we have all arranged to go out to dinner tonight." "Then I will put champagne on ice and you will come straight to my arms after you have eaten with your friends" Laurent insisted. "I will not take no for an answer and I have something very beautiful to give you!" "All right Laurent, I'll come" I laughed. "How could any woman refuse a Frenchman bearing gifts?" "Ah c'est bon, the hours will seem like days until you are with me" he sighed. "I will expect you in my suite at 10.30; au revoir my darling." An hour later an even larger bouquet of roses arrived.

By seven o'clock, I had packed in readiness for the journey to Kuala Lumpur. We all enjoyed an early glass of champagne on the veranda and the taxi arrived at 7.30. It was lovely to sit in the back of the car in between Julie and

Diane and spend the next five minutes giggling like schoolgirls. "Are you going to sleep with him?" Julie whispered. "Gosh if I was single I'd be there like a shot!"

"Who's been shot?" asked Mickey, from the front seat. "I said it's very hot!" Lied Julie and we all burst into fits of laughter. But was I going to sleep with him? That really was difficult to say. Laurent was one of the most physically attractive men I had ever met and I was very tempted to abandon myself to a night of pure passion! But then there was Dominic, he had confused everything. The fact of the matter was, I was still in love with a twenty one year old Marine. The new Dominic was a married stranger in his mid-forties! By the time we had arrived at the restaurant I had made up my mind!

The restaurant was one of Micky's favourites and specialised in Thai fish dishes and rice. The place was spotless and the service excellent which, when added to the most pleasant company could not have been more perfect. At 10.15 we hailed separate taxis and went off in opposite directions. As the car inched its way through the busy streets I found myself overcome with a mixture of excited anticipation and guilt. Why on earth should I feel guilty about spending the night with Laurent? "My God, you're a grown women without ties, go and have a bloody good time!" I told myself angrily.

I entered Raffles Hotel and headed straight for the powder room. I swallowed hard and ran a hairbrush through my long hair. A touch of pink lipstick and a quick puff of my favourite perfume put the confidence back. I left the powder room and stepped into the lift. I stepped out of the lift to find Laurent already waiting at his door, a huge flashing white smile spreading over his face. My knees felt a little weak as he took my hand and kissed it most gently. "I want tonight to be very special," he said softly, as he led me into the luxurious suite and to a large Chinese silk sofa. He had selected the most wonderful French love songs that floated around the room like soothing waves. The champagne cork flew almost in slow motion and we filled our glasses with the fizzing golden liquid. "We must stay awake all night making love and then we will watch the sun rise." Laurent whispered. "I do not want to miss a second of the time we have together by sleeping." I put the palm of my hand gently on his cheek and then slowly traced the outline of his mouth with my fingertips. He took my hand in his and kissed the inside of my fingers as if they were the most delicate things he had ever held. He took the glass gently from my other hand and simultaneously began to kiss my neck and shoulders. My whole body ached and trembled with longing and I returned his kisses with a passion long since forgotten. We made love on that big silk sofa and the world slipped away into a wonderful glowing haze. Much later we wrapped ourselves in sheets and curled up with cushions on the floor to wait for the sun to rise. We talked and talked through the night softly and with a new found belonging. He worried about not being around to protect me over the next two weeks and I reassured him with kisses. As the sun rose I knew that I was going to miss him terribly and when he slipped the gold locket around my neck, I really believed that I might be in love with him.

I arrived back at the house with just an hour to spare before Dominic was to arrive. Diane rushed me into the kitchen to get the news and then whizzed me to the breakfast table where the others waited eagerly. When Dominic arrived he was greeted by a huddle of tearful women and sad looking children. I promised to come back to see Julie and Micky before returning to England and climbed up into the waiting Jeep. "You look exhausted" said Dominic, as we drove away from the little waving group of smiling faces. "I hope you had a good night's sleep, we have a long drive ahead of us!"

Chapter 13

Waves of tiredness started to hit me long before we had reached the Causeway, which was to take us across to Malaya. Even early in the morning the heat was oppressive and it was not helping me in the least. I was quite excited about the idea of Malaya, visiting the places where my father had plied his murderous trade and really wanted to see and absorb everything. "There's a flask of black coffee behind the seat" Dominic said suddenly, "you obviously had a rough night!" Gratefully I reached for the flask as Dominic slowed down to enable the operation of coffee pouring to be done reasonably smoothly. I passed the cup to Dominic who without hesitation took one long gulp and handed it back to me. Accidentally, I almost clasped his hand sending the most disturbing tingling sensation to my feet. Dominic was, however, outwardly unruffled, but remained silent for the next five minutes. During this time I found myself taking discreet sideways glances at the man who I had loved and lost all those years ago. His deeply tanned arms and legs were those of a fit and extremely healthy sportsman. His hands were so familiar and I remembered clearly loving the way he kept his nails very clean and regularly clipped. They were the kind of strong manly hands that gave one confidence and in my case, reach out for. His face had weathered in a handsome, rugged way and despite myself, I realised that I still found him very attractive indeed. "We'll be crossing the Causeway in the next couple of minutes" Dominic said rather quietly and then proceeded to give me a potted history of when and how the Causeway was built. It seemed only minutes before we were entering the mysterious country of Malaya and I felt that at last the adventure was really beginning. The whole journey was a good 300 miles distant and Dominic had proposed that we stay overnight in Malacca. There was no point in travelling during the hottest part of the day and it made sense for me to spend a few hours there purely out of interest.

Dominic explained that it was well over two thousand years ago when the ancestors of the people who are now called Malays first reached the peninsula. They had come very slowly from central Asia, mingling with Chinese tribes on the way. At that time they may have been white, some of them still are. Most have skins of very pale brown or olive tint. These people did not stop moving when they reached the southern tip of the mainland. Some of them crossed to the islands of Indonesia and established strong kingdoms in Sumatra and Java. For several centuries, the Kings of Sumatra also ruled the mainland people and when Sumatra was conquered by its neighbour Java (about AD 1400) its king fled to what is now the mainland port of Malacca. There he began a new kingdom, which today is one of the fourteen states of Malaysia.

We passed through many scattered villages where wooden houses were built in no obvious order or arrangement. Occasionally a neat row of houses could be seen that were built on the ground and not on stilts as were the majority. Dominic explained that these were Chinese settlements, whereas the native Malays built their houses randomly on stilts. After about an hour and a half the Jeep turned down a dusty track and pulled up outside a Chinese house. A carefully tended garden surrounded the house, which adjoined a little plantation of coconut palms, bananas, mango and durian. To the north a small field of tapioca had been planted and family rice fields could be glimpsed stretching up into the hillside. I imagined it to be a very beautiful place to live. "This is Chor Ling's brother's house" Dominic explained. "I always call in for refreshment when out this way, you'll like him. He is a typically proud Chinese who looks after his family well and works very hard in the fields producing all his own vegetables, grains and rice." Dominic sounded the horn and waited. After a few minutes a small grey haired Chinaman came rushing out from the behind the house, followed by two younger men. We climbed down from the Jeep and walked forward to greet them. A great deal of bowing, smiling and shaking of hands took place and we were hastened through the dark interior of the house and out onto a rear wooden veranda. Chor Sen motioned for me to sit in what was obviously the bamboo chair especially kept for visitors, handed me a large faded fan and nodded approvingly. The two younger men sat together on a wooden bench smiling nervously in my direction and I realised that they were identical twins. "Joanna, this is Bill and Ben" announced Dominic. Their parents gave them these nicknames after Andy Pandy's two friends the Flower Pot Men! They speak good English but are a little shy of strangers. Their mother died when they were only three so they have been brought up by Chor Sen alone."

"It is a pleasure to meet you" I said, smiling as broadly as possible whilst waving the fan gently in front of my face. Bill and Ben spent the next hour taking in turns to describe what they had been doing over the last few months since Dominic's last visit. I heard how a dispute with a Malayan neighbour had resulted in the authorities denying access to the Malayan family over one of Chor Sen's fields. This had resulted in a violent scuffle between the men of each family. Dominic explained that minor disputes still existed between different groups that stemmed from a history of tribal fighting over several hundred years. In general, however, Malays and Chinese Indians lived quite contentedly alongside each other.

As we continued our journey north, Dominic told me how the Malays were once an unruly people. They had long been feared as pirates, as ready to rob each other as anyone else. So the people of adjoining villages would band together for mutual protection. A local leader would emerge and he would become a Sultan - a title that made me think of Arabian nights.

"What made you decide to settle in Malaya rather than another part of Malaysia?" I asked. "I liked the country and the people" Dominic said, without hesitation. "Life is very easy for the Malays. The climate is so regular that a farmer need only work for two months of the year to earn enough to support his family. When he plants rice he knows to within a day or two when the rains will come. He also knows that the sun will shine for most of the year, so that a good harvest is assured. I also became fascinated by the history of the area and decided to return here when I left the Marines."

"Would you ever consider returning to England?" I asked. "I had no reason to stay in England then and I have no reason to return in the future," he snapped and lapsed into an agitated silence. Dominic's moods swung in the most unpredictable way, so I decided to look at the view for a while. I must have dozed because we were suddenly driving through a densely populated area. The sound of ships could be heard hooting their way into port and at last we had reached Malacca. That night, I slept like a log, which was not surprising after the long hot day and the lack of sleep the night before. That was up until the arrival of my nocturnal visitor.

Earlier, Dominic had driven us into the old part of the town close to the docks where we repaired to a British club with accommodation. British planters and traders mingled with Malays in their colourful skirts and blouses, Indians in their longer saris and robes, Europeans and smartly dressed Chinese. The club had apparently changed very little over the last twenty years where whisky and beer continued to be drunk under slow turning fans. I got the feeling that Dominic was enjoying being seen in my company and this was apparent by the way acquaintances standing next to him at the bar, patted his back whilst nodding in my direction. Also by the way he walked towards me with the drinks, cocky to say the least. Mind you, I was obviously not supposed to notice this male to male telepathy and smiled sweetly as if I was oblivious to the whole thing. Food then became the most pressing issue as we were both pretty hungry. Pork with everything seemed the most popular item on the menu, however, to the proprietor's disgust I chose a vegetable risotto instead. By the end of the day Dominic had no choice but to virtually carry me to my room. I vaguely recalled a certain amount of enthusiastic male whistling as we left the bar, but mostly I was acutely aware of the closeness of Dominic's body as he lifted me onto the bed. "I suppose you're too drunk to undress yourself!" Dominic had groaned. "I'll ask Annie the Proprietors wife to give you a hand." "No, no" I had foolishly slurred, "you can undress me, after all, you have seen it all before!"

He did, rather angrily remove my clothes leaving me in my bra and pants and then covered me with a sheet. I remembered giggling rather a lot and then hearing the door slam. The Dominic I used to know would definitely not have been such a gentleman!

Chapter 14

"Joanna, wake up!" I blearily heard Dominic's voice breaking into my deep sleep. His hands were now firmly on my shoulders and he had started to gently shake me awake. "What time is it, it's still dark!" I groaned. "Go away!" "Joanna, you must wake up" Dominic said quietly but very firmly, "there's someone here to see you!"

"What, here in my room?" I gasped sitting bolt upright and peering into the gloom. "Keep your voice down" hissed Dominic, "Abdul has come under cover of darkness and he must leave before it gets light. If he is caught talking to us he could be a dead man!"

Dominic's vague silhouette moved towards the window and deftly closed the curtains. The light from the lamp was blinding and my eyes took a while to adjust. Abdul stood just inside the door and bowed politely before reaching for a chair. I suddenly realised that his widening grin had everything to do with my semi-naked appearance and I quickly pulled the sheet around me. Dominic quietly explained that, before leaving Singapore, he had made contact with a retired Commander of the British Army, who had been based in Kuala Lumpur at the same time as the Prince. He had known the Prince well and his English friend Major Worme. Abdul was a young recruit who became the Prince's batman and served with him during the 50's and 60's. The Commander had included Abdul within a small group of friends who regularly met to play bridge. However, Abdul had been sworn to secrecy and never once imparted any information about the Prince's activities nor that of his English friend Major Worme. When the Prince retired from the army he returned to his father's house in Kuala Lumpur. Abdul, despite having served nearly twenty years with the Prince was thrown aside and forced to accept a lowly private's position. If anyone was willing to help in providing information and to fill in the sizeable gaps in the annals of history, Abdul was our man. The Commander had sent word to Abdul that we would be in Malacca and invited him to pay us a call. *"You must understand,"* Abdul began in perfect English *"that I am here because I want the truth to be known. My wife and family have suffered over many years because I had devoted a large part of my life to the Prince, who left me on a lowly private's pay with a wife and four children to support. After just a few short years I was invalided out of the army and made homeless. The Prince refused to help me and even threatened to have me killed if I were to bother him again. The Commander found me somewhere to live and I eventually found work here in Malacca."*

I was now wide awake and absolutely intrigued. I reached for my bag and tape recorder and encouraged Abdul to continue. Abdul shifted in his seat and quickly pulled out a rather grey handkerchief and wiped his brow. He had a small thin swarthy appearance with a rather oversized drooping moustache, which he constantly twirled around his fore finger. He had strong Arabic features, but with the small slanted eyes of the Chinese. His hair was thinning and greying and I put him probably in his late fifties.

"When Major Worme first arrived on the scene," he continued *"I had no reason to suspect him of being anything other than an old friend from England. He was, however, an insatiable philanderer and I became most concerned that the Prince may be mixing with the wrong company. He, the Prince, had married one of the most desirable women in Malaysia and even she was not safe from Worme's advances. The Prince refused to believe me when I warned him that this was the case and he threatened to have me flogged if I ever mentioned it again. The Prince was a fool and was completely mesmerised by the man."* Abdul once again wiped his brow and I motioned to Dominic to pass him a glass of bottled water. Over the next hour we learnt that Abdul had been shocked to find out the real reason for Major Worme being in Malaya. He had been taken to Worme's room the night before the first assassination and told that he would be accompanying the two men to Perai. He was sworn to secrecy under threat of his wife having her throat cut, should he ever say a word to anyone. It also turned

out that in my farmhouse garden the Prince had been very economical with the truth. He and my father had set out not only to kill selected targets; they had also planned to make themselves very rich in the process. After my father had shot dead the target, the men would set about killing the rest of the entourage making sure that at least one woman was left to ravage before killing her too! Then the pillaging began with the Prince and my father pocketing the most expensive items of jewellery. I reached for my bag and found the photograph of the diamond and ruby necklace. I passed it to Abdul who looked at it closely. *"Yes"* said Abdul immediately, *"this belonged to a very rich sultan who trusted the Prince totally. The Prince lured him into the palace gardens whilst I was to steal the necklace from the Sultans bedroom safe. The Sultan had already opened it to show the Prince his jewels, that's how much of a fool the man was. As soon as I had the necklace I returned to the garden room and gave the Prince the nod. Seconds later the shot rang out and the Sultan lay dead on the ground. The Prince was a very good actor, he screamed and shouted for the palace guards and even wept openly over his 'friend's' body!"*

At some time during the last few minutes, Dominic had sat on the bed and put a comforting arm around my bare shoulders. This show of concern was quite unnerving and I found myself almost self-consciously mumbling something about 'being all right'. He removed his arm but stayed sat beside me on the bed. "When did you last see George Worme?" Dominic asked. Abdul shifted in his seat again and continued. *"In 1969, the Prince retired from the Army and moved back to Kuala Lumpur. Worme was invited to join them, from England, to celebrate the Prince's new status and to complete one last assassination. After the killing, the Prince and Worme gunned down the men who had faithfully followed them for nearly twenty years and then turned on me. Quite rightly, the Prince knew well enough that the threat to my family was so great that I was bound to keep my mouth shut. Worme stayed on for another month, lording it as usual amongst the expats and the rich society. I was the only one who knew of*

Worme's affair with the Princess and where the stolen jewellery was kept. Worme promised that he would make it worth my while if I was to arrange accommodation for them in Singapore and to pack the diamond and ruby necklace in the Princess's bag. She went on ahead on the pretence of a shopping trip to Hong Kong. Worme left a week later and as instructed I put the letter from the Princess on her dressing table."

"Did you not hear from either of them again?" I asked, desperately needing to know their movements during the next six months. *"I had booked them into Raffles Hotel for two weeks," Abdul said, shaking his head. "Although Worme had promised to help me, I heard nothing until her coffin arrived six months later. Immediately after the Prince had read the letter from his wife he dismissed me. The army found me a miserable job in their kitchens, so I was out of touch with the family after that."*

A small glimmer of light was squeezing its way through the curtains and Abdul sprang to his feet. He quickly reached inside his shirt and produced a small leather bound book, which he passed to Dominic. *"It is getting light, I must go. You will find all the evidence you need in there. I recorded every assassination in detail, perhaps now history can be rewritten with the truth. Knowing that Worme is dead and that the Prince is on his death bed, I feel relatively safe. However, my need for self-preservation will always be with me, so I must leave before it gets too light."*

I wrapped myself tightly in the sheet and walked Abdul to the door. My heart went out to him knowing how he had suffered over so many years and I shook his hand warmly. I switched out the light and quietly opened the door to watch him silently disappear into the gloom of the passageway. I turned to find Dominic right behind me. "We may as well get another hours sleep" he said. "I'll meet you downstairs at 7.30 for breakfast." And he was gone. I walked over to the window, opened the curtains and looked out to see the first signs of the sunrise. I could just make out the masts of ships and the great arms of the derricks stretching out over the docks. I was wide awake over the next hour and eventually decided on a shower and an early morning walk before breakfast. If I could find a phone I could also ring home to check on Emma and Harry who now seemed to be a million miles away.

Chapter 15

Dominic angrily thumped the coffee pot onto the breakfast table after filling our cups. "I would have credited you with more intelligence!" he barked. "All I did was walk down to the wharf to look at the ships!" I said defensively. "Besides, I needed to find a telephone; this dreadful place doesn't have one."

"If you had spoken to me first, I would have arranged for you to use the proprietor's phone, for God's sake!" he bellowed. Then realising that we were drawing the attention from the other two people in the room, he lowered his voice. "Joanna, you are in Malacca not Exmouth" he continued. "You should never go prancing off on your own in a place like this, especially when it is still not properly light, you could have been raped and murdered!"

"I am perfectly capable of taking care of myself!" I retaliated, waving my rape alarm under his nose. "Look, Joanna" he said gently "If we are to work together successfully then it is essential that we communicate with each other at all times don't you agree? Aren't those things illegal?"

I felt the smile spread over my face as I realised that he had been genuinely worried, the man actually did still care at least a little bit. On the other hand perhaps it was his fee he was more concerned about! I chose to believe the former. "I would like to use the proprietor's phone before we leave, I didn't actually find one," I said rather weakly.

Whilst Dominic went up to the rooms to collect our bags, Annie showed me into the little dusty office and sat me down with a rather antiquated telephone. "Mum, where on earth are you?" Squealed a very excited Emma. "I've burnt my shoulders out in the garden and I couldn't find any 'after sun' anywhere! Finny has been in trouble with the farmer next door, he only wanted to play with the lambs. Anyway, he's calmed down now and is sleeping a lot under the Chestnut Tree with Dippy. Those new throws I bought have to be dry cleaned, but I'm sure that they could be washed, they are pure cotton....."

"Emma, Emma!" I shouted down the line, "I'm using someone else's phone here, can I answer the first question please?" "Oops, sorry Mum" she said sweetly. "We do miss you and now I hear from Julie that you've headed off into the Jungle with a hunky big game hunter!"

"Partly right" I laughed, then realised with a stab to my heart that she was talking about her own father. "We're about to leave Malacca and head on up to Kuala Lumpur" I said, trying to sound as calm as possible. "Things are progressing very well and my research is proving fascinating. I'll be staying with Dominic and his wife for at least a week, so I will ring you again when I get there." "What a pity" Said Emma, "so the hunk is married, so much for the love interest!" "Actually darling, I have met someone," I found myself saying. "He's a French fashion designer called Laurent. We've become very good friends and I shall be seeing him again when I return to Singapore."

Dominic's frame filled the doorway and it was obvious that he had overheard the last sentence. His eyes flashed with anger and his shoulders had widened to an alarming degree. "I must go darling" I said to Emma, "Dominic's ready to leave, I'll ring you again from Kuala Lumpur."

I followed Dominic out to the Jeep and watched him throw our bags into the back. I climbed in and we lurched forward even before I had managed to fasten my seat belt. I could feel his hostility like a hot knife in the throat and resolved to say nothing until he had calmed down. In no time at all we were leaving Malacca behind and heading out onto the open road. The plan was to reach Kuala Lumpur by tea-time, with a break along the way. The road took us away from the coast and the countryside became dense jungle stretching away from us up into the mountains. It had rained overnight and the trees steamed like smouldering volcanoes. Dominic eventually relaxed a little and put a classical tape on. "Are you sleeping with this Laurent person?" He said out of the blue. "That is none of your business!" I said rather pathetically as my voice caught in my throat. "Well, it's obvious that you are" he sneered. "I'm disappointed in your exceptionally poor taste."

At this point I felt overwhelmed with a mixture of anger and desperation. I battled mentally with the ridiculous feeling of guilt I felt and found myself lying as if I had been unfaithful! "I am not sleeping with him" I stormed, "but don't think that I haven't thought about it, because I have!"

The night that I had spent with Laurent had been heaven. As we lay on the floor with cushions under our heads, watching the sun slowly rise, nothing else in the world had mattered. Even thoughts of Dominic had been washed away with the sheer romance of the occasion. I felt for the locket at my throat and closed my eyes; there was no way Dominic was going to take the wonder of that night away from me. "So you have children?" Dominic asked just as suddenly as the previous question. "I assume that you were not telling your husband about your French lover!"

"I am not married and Emma is my only child, do you want to talk about her?" I asked rather surprised at the sudden interest. Dominic scowled. "As you have already pointed out your personal life is none of my business." And with that sarcastic comment he turned up the music and lapsed into silence until we finally reached a small Malay village with a bright bustling market.

The smell of cooking wafted over from a small covered stall and we purchased two bowls of fresh egg noodles in a chilli sauce. Despite the heat they were delicious and we followed this with fresh slices of watermelon. Dominic talked freely with a number of villagers who nodded, bowed and smiled broadly in my direction. Two hours later we were entering the magnificent city of Kuala Lumpur, the place that had haunted my dreams for the last three weeks. Dominic had explained that Kuala Lumpur had the best university in Malaysia. He was proud to be associated with it and to occasionally lecture history students in their final years. Most of the people in Malaya are Muslims and that is why the university buildings were built to resemble a beautiful mosque. Many modern apartments also existed to house the students and lecturers. As the building came into view, the golden domes shone like welcoming beacons in the sunshine. The Jeep wound its way between thoroughly modern and some rather tacky buildings until we finally headed out into the countryside. Dominic had built his own villa, a mile outside of the city, which had been completed just five years ago. I was keen to see what kind of home the new Dominic had designed for himself.... and Susie. As we turned down a dusty track and through an area of jungle I felt a severe attack of anxiety take over. It was not the house that I was nervous about, it was the woman to whom Dominic had pledged his life to, his wife Susie! Suddenly we came to a halt in front of a pair of high black and gold ornate gates. Dominic reached for a remote control and pointed it at the gates that swung slowly away from us. We drove past a smiling peak capped gentlemen, onto a pale gravel Drive, and through a small area of jungle to the house. Dominic sounded the horn as we pulled up in front of the large white painted villa. It was absolutely beautiful! A wide veranda stretched along the whole front of the house, which spilled over, with tubs of flowers and shrubs. Dominic leapt out of the Jeep and ran to greet an apparition of beauty who flung herself into his arms and kissed and hugged him until I was sure he would suffocate. Taking her hand he brought her towards me smiling broadly with delighted pride. I swallowed hard, slid down to the ground and managed a shaky smile. "Joanna, I want you to meet my beautiful Susie," he said proudly. "Susie this is Joanna Wilde."

I could not believe my eyes; Susie was incredibly beautiful, taller than the average Chinese with waist length golden brown hair. Her features were Malay, but with a definite trace of European and her eyes were blue. Worst of all she was less than half my age! "Come with me Joanna!" she said, excitedly grabbing my hand. "I've made up the guest bedroom for you overlooking the lake. Dominic dug it out himself because he wanted to attract the many water birds in the area. He is heavily into natural history as well you know!"

Overwhelmed by the welcome I found it hard not to immediately like Susie. She never ceased to smile and was so pleased to have a woman to talk to that I found myself enthusiastically following her every footstep! Her English was perfect, almost no trace of an accent but then she did speak several languages. The villa was absolutely delightful and Susie's feminine influence was everywhere from the tumbling pots of flowers to the Laura Ashley wallpaper and chintz curtains. Yes, Dominic had given her free reign to choose the soft furnishings but he was in charge of the landscaping and of course his own personal study. Following tea overlooking the lake we suddenly remembered the bags. We all walked out to the Jeep because Dominic had mentioned a present for Susie and she could not contain her excitement. Dominic opened the rear door of the Jeep and reached for the first bag.

Chapter 16

A white, almost transparent, blood stained hand slid out from under the canvas and hung stiffly over the back of the jeep! Susie gasped and grabbed my arm and I grabbed Dominic's. The silence was deafening as we huddled together in a state of frozen shock, until Dominic gently released my grip and leant over the canvas. He removed the rest of the bags and placed them on the ground. With utmost care he slowly lifted the corner of the canvas and we watched in horror as Abdul's lifeless body was revealed. His throat had been cut from ear to ear and his mouth hung wide open in a fixed scream. I felt Susie become heavy beside me and just managed to prevent her from falling as she fainted. Dominic hastily replaced the canvas but not before Abdul's head had rolled to one side staring at me through wide sightless eyes. My shock turned to despair as I realised that it was my fault the poor unhappy man had been brutally murdered. Fighting back the tears, I held tightly onto the moaning Susie as she started to come round. Dominic rushed to my aid and quickly took Susie up into his arms and headed for the house. I stumbled after them feeling horribly vulnerable and took several fearful glances around me before closing and locking the door. Dominic had lain Susie on a large soft sofa in the sitting room and was reaching for the brandy bottle. I grabbed three glasses from the sideboard and joined him. In silence he filled the glasses and took one over to Susie. His love for her was so obvious, as he gently raised her head and placed the glass to her lips. She choked on the first mouthful then managed to swallow, until at last she was sitting upright looking extremely pale and frightened. "I'm so..so sorry." I found myself stammering. "This is all my fault. I should never have got you involved and now I've put you both in danger."

"Sit down and calm yourself!" Dominic said firmly but not unkindly. "If anyone is to blame it's that bastard father of yours. Even from the grave he is still destroying lives. I was well aware that in taking this job we might open up a few cans of worms, if you'll excuse the pun!"

"This really isn't a time for jokes Dominic, what on earth are we going to do with Abdul? If we call the police, how are we going to explain ourselves?" "Firstly, we are all going to sit down and finish our brandies," he said calmly.

I sank wearily down into a large leather armchair and swallowed the golden liquid in one. Dominic sat with his arm around Susie who was now fully compos mentis. Then, as if fate was taking a hand, the door burst open and a beautiful golden Labrador rushed eagerly across the room and sat panting beside me. His big brown eyes gazed adoringly up at me and I knew in an instant that what I really needed was to smooth and hug a dog. Whenever I felt stressful, Dippy would always be there to provide the calming lick and warm body to hug. This beautiful dog at my feet had obviously got the same message.

"Meet Satan" said Dominic enthusiastically. "We inherited him from expats who were returning to England. He and the guard dogs are on very good terms despite the fact that Satan is spoilt beyond belief and is allowed to live in the house. We are very secure here, by the way, my grounds men are also trained ex-servicemen and we have six guard dogs. There is little chance of any one getting into the grounds without an invitation!"

I felt a great wave of relief came over me. For the first time I looked around the room and realised that we were surrounded by a number of priceless artefacts, paintings and furniture. Dominic had obviously done extremely well for himself, which was not particularly surprising remembering the young man with a strong belief in his own potential. He had obviously travelled extensively and collected many beautiful and fascinating things on the way. I looked back at the handsome sun-tanned man and saw the love and concern on his face as he quietly talked to Susie.

"Susie is fine now," he smiled talking to me. "I'm going outside to have a word with the men, perhaps you might like to run a bath and freshen up." He kissed Susie on the forehead and left the room followed by the enthusiastic Satan.

Susie smiled, reached for my hand and guided me back along the corridors and up a wide flight of marble stairs to an enormous bathroom. "Dominic had the bath shipped over from England" Susie said proudly. "He isn't very fond of the modern stuff. If you prefer a shower there is an ensuite attached to the main bedroom at the far end of this corridor, I'll show you. I prefer to use the bathroom but the choice is yours."

I felt as if I was intruding as we entered the main bedroom. Dominic had flung his bags on the king size bed which had obviously been carefully made that morning. The room was not as feminine as I expected although continued the theme of tasteful quality to be found in the rest of the house. Fresh flowers adorned the dressing table but other than this, there was little evidence of the room being anything but functional. "You don't have to walk through the bedroom if you don't want to" Susie explained. "There's a separate entrance off the corridor if you prefer." I decided to have a soak in the bath, besides Dominic may want to use the shower room himself shortly. Susie had insisted that I help myself to any of the oils or bath foams displayed all around the large lion footed tub. I selected a little of everything then sat and watched the rushing water as it slowly filled the tub. My thoughts went back to Abdul and tears sprung into my eyes again as the lump grew once more in my throat. The Prince had carried out his threat despite being on his deathbed; one way or another I was determined to make him pay for what he had done. Hopefully, the leather bound book that Abdul had handed to Dominic would provide all the ammunition we might need. I decided to make a start on reading it first thing in the morning. I undressed, slid down into the warm bubbling water and under the surface. The whole of my body was immersed in the great length of the bath and the depth of the water. After a few seconds I raised my head and slowly surfaced letting the water level drop a little. I felt his presence before I had opened my eyes and subsequently kept my shoulders below the foaming surface.

"You still have that mole on your neck," Dominic stated matter of factly.

"You're not as skinny as you were but you are in pretty good shape despite that."

"Dominic, what are you doing in here?" I said weakly. "What would Susie think?"

"Oh, she's in the kitchen discussing dinner with Mrs Lee," he chuckled. "I wanted to have a quiet chat with you and this seemed like a good moment."

The warm water had started to relax my tense muscles, however, it was also helping to arouse the old stirring of desire below the surface of the water. Dominic pulled over a bamboo stool and perched himself, knees apart in his shorts for God's sake, just feet away from me! "I'm not so sure that this is a good moment Dominic, I was going to have a doze for ten minutes or so." "Don't worry, I won't stay long," he smiled that old familiar smile. "I've discussed with the men the best option for disposing of Abdul's body. The Prince has returned to his house in Kuala Lumpur and is confined to bed, however, he is obviously still in control and is visited daily by his son Hussein. Apparently, he's creating a great deal of washing and is demanding fresh bedding every day, which means that laundry is collected and delivered regularly. I have ordered a van from the same laundry firm to collect a load of washing from here this evening, however, they won't be collecting laundry! My men can rely on the driver to deliver the laundry basket straight to the Prince's house and to deposit it in his utility room. The body will be discovered by a member of his domestic staff, also on our payroll, who will immediately ring the police! Let's see how the Prince gets out of that one!"

"Oh, Dominic that's brilliant news," I said, greatly relieved. "Is there anything I can do to help?" "The most helpful thing you could do is to join us for pre-dinner drinks at 7 O'clock and entertain Susie. She is really keen to hear about British fashions and such like. Oh yes, and you might like to wear something that will cover up those raised nipples!"

I looked down at the surface of the water and was horrified to see two neatly rounded circles of bubble free water and a pair of nipples standing proudly just above the surface. I grabbed a large soaking sponge and threw it at the retreating Dominic, catching him neatly on his right buttock with an almighty thwack! He picked up the sponge and advanced back towards me. Laughing he handed it back to me and warned me to behave myself in future or I might be contravening our business arrangement! Then with an exaggerated swagger he left the room. The ice had at last melted!

Chapter 17

Susie had thought of everything, bottled water, perfumed tissues and a hair dryer plugged in and ready for use. More fresh flowers adorned the glass topped dressing table and a silver brush and comb set was laid neatly on a pretty mother of pearl tray. I sat on the matching stool and looked around the room through the reflection in the mirror. Long lace curtains blew gently in and out, framing the double doors that led out onto a welcoming balcony. I slipped into a sarong and walked out to look at the view. Sure enough, there was the man-made lake already surrounded by maturing trees and flowering shrubs. Wild birds of many colours ducked and dived on the surface of the water and a chorus of birdsong filled the air. The place was an absolute dream; I could have been very happy there if things had been different. Having dried my hair, I slipped into a cool white cotton frock and placed a colourful Alice band in my hair. Now that Dominic and I seemed to be on better terms I felt this feminine but not too sexy outfit would be appropriate for dinner in the company of his sweet wife. It was obvious that Dominic had completely relaxed because he had returned to the place where he was most happy. Despite the horrifying discovery of Abdul's body, he was totally in control and now in his element. I had to now make a conscious effort to accept the circumstances and to concentrate on research; if this meant burying my still strong emotions for the man then so be it.

"So, what will you have?" asked a smiling Dominic, waving an empty glass at me from across the other side of the sitting room. I decided on a long cool glass of spritzer with ice and turned to watch the enthusiastic Susie come gliding into the room in the most beautiful blue silk shift and matching trousers. Dominic beamed an approving smile and put his arm protectively round her shoulders. "I hope you don't mind" said Susie, "but I've invited four friends from University to join us for dinner. Dominic insisted that we also invite someone of his own age so Charlie and Anne Webber are coming too." Dominic smiled. "Susie is studying languages, history and English in KL and I'm told that she is an exceptional pupil. Charlie is a Zoologist and is a full time lecturer there; he and Anne are English by the way. Anne is a part-time tennis coach and she and Charlie are also very strong squash players. Ah, someone is arriving now!"

Charlie had to be seen to be believed! He marched into the sitting room wearing old corduroys, short sleeved tennis shirt, a misshapen sleeveless green sweater and a well holed pair of scruffy trainers. He carried a bottle of wine in his left hand and a squash racket in his right. He was reed thin but wiry and obviously extremely fit, however, his pallor was very pale considering the climate he lived in. Anne, on the other hand, though also very slim, was nut brown and her hair had been bleached blond by the hours spent out in the sun. She was a little shy, but nevertheless began to loosen up once she had consumed her second glass of wine. She apologised for her husband's unkempt appearance, but had abandoned trying to smarten him up several years ago!

Susie's four friends consisted of two girls, one black American and one English. The two young men were both Malayan. The company was therefore very cosmopolitan and the conversation proved most absorbing. After a most delicious meal cooked and presented by the very valuable Mrs Lee, we repaired to the garden to watch Charlie playing ghost shots with his squash racket. Finding this a little boring, I began a lengthy conversation with Anne. They had known Dominic for three years; he and Charlie had a regular "knock" on the squash court. Despite their ages, Charlie was also in his forties, they both played in the Malayan league representing Kuala Lumpur. It also turned out that Dominic was a highly rated tennis player and held regular tournaments here at the house. I discovered that he had built a suburb fitness centre in the grounds to the east of the house, which included swimming pool, tennis courts, squash court and gymnasium! She understood that he had made most of his money arranging export finance and something called mergers and acquisitions. He also had a major shareholding in a machine parts company in Singapore.

She and I were sat in the shade of a small group of coconut palms from where we could see that the ghosting had ended and Susie was setting out croquet hoops. The sun had sunk fairly low in the sky, however, there would be time for at least one round before it was dark. "Miss Wilde, there is a telephone call for you." Mrs Lee said, as unobtrusively as possible. "A Mr DuPont." "Tell him she's busy!" Dominic's sudden fierce interruption caused the company to fall into stunned silence. Realising that he had raised a few eyebrows, he lowered his voice and turned to me. "I would suggest that you call him back tomorrow, we do have guests after all."

"Dominic!" Susie's surprised voice intervened. "Joanna is also a guest, I would have thought that she could make up her own mind as to whether she wants to take the call or not."

"Thank you Susie," I smiled. "You are absolutely right." I stood, brushed past the glowering Dominic and walked into the house. As I reached for the receiver, I could hear the silence being broken by Susie encouraging everyone to take up a mallet. Suddenly, I felt very apprehensive and found myself stammering down the phone, I hadn't spoken to Laurent since that morning after the night before!

"Hi, hi Laurent it's good to, to hear from you."

"But that is not a very romantic greeting for the man who would give his life for you, who adores the very ground you walk on! Is everything all right, is that pig of an Englishman not treating you well? I will kill him with my bare hands should he upset you in any way, I really mean it!"

I sat down on the silk lined chair next to the phone and smiled. "Dear Laurent, a women could not be more enchanted by your genuine concern. Please do not worry, everything here is fine. We have just had dinner with a number of delightful people and I will be getting on with an intensive amount of research first thing in the morning."

"So, what have you discovered so far, any trace of the necklace yet?" Laurent sounded curious. "Absolutely no trace at all, however, we do have an interesting book now which contains a lot of information regarding the assassinations." "What sort of book, where did you get it from?"

The telephone receiver was wrenched from my grasp and Dominic, red faced and boiling with anger, stood defiantly beside me. "For God's sake woman, you'll be telling him about Abdul next are you completely stupid?" Shocked, I tried to snatch the receiver back but before I could do so he had slammed it down into its socket. Now I was really mad! "How dare you, who the bloody hell do you think you are? I have no secrets from Laurent, he loves me and I love him. Don't you ever do anything like that again!" "Now the truth is really coming out, I knew he was your lover. He's got you so enmeshed in his web that you are prepared to risk the lives of all those around you!" I shook my head in disbelief and felt tears begin to prick my eyes. "I know Laurent well enough to be able to trust him totally!" I lied. "Oh, really! Then how come that he has access to my ex-directory number, where do you suppose he got that from?" Dominic fumed. Suddenly the phone rang again, I raised my hand to prevent Dominic from saying another word. "Joanna, is that you? We seemed to have got cut off!" Laurent's concerned voice came through the wires. "Yes it's me, I don't know what happened but at least we're connected again" I tried to sound calm. "By the way Laurent, how did you get this number?" There was a pregnant pause at the other end. "Your friend in Singapore gave it to me, Julie isn't it? Why do you ask, the most important thing is that I could not wait to hear your voice and so I rang her for the number."

I smiled with relief and gave Dominic the thumbs up. "I should have realised that you would find the number somehow, no matter how difficult! But I can't really talk now, Laurent, as we have visitors and it's impolite to ignore them for too long. Give me your number and I will ring you tomorrow evening." "No, no" Laurent purred. "I will ring you at say 7 O'clock. Till then my darling, je taime, je taime!"

I replaced the receiver and looked Dominic straight in the face. "There was nothing sinister about Laurent having this number" I announced triumphantly. "Julie gave it to him, does that satisfy you?" "It certainly does!" Dominic put his hand on my shoulder and with his face no further than six inches from my own said, "Julie has never had this number, she only has my office number in Singapore. I ring in daily to the office to see if there are any messages, not even my personal assistant has this number!"

And with that last angry outburst he turned and stormed back out into the garden. I stood in frozen silence for several minutes before I was finally brought back to reality by a gentle warm wet tongue on my ankle. Satan's big brown eyes looked up at me with real concern, I sat down on the floor and hugged his warm comforting body. He licked my chin and my tears dripped slowly into his golden fur.

Chapter 18

I stepped through the study door and found myself in a different world. Almost every bit of wall in this vast room was covered from floor to ceiling in bookshelves, and where there weren't any books the spaces were filled by souvenirs of Dominic's world travels. The far end of the room boasted a huge inglenook stone fireplace with a massive oak lintel. Above the fireplace hung the largest South Pacific tappa cloth I had ever seen, threaded at the top and bottom by giant bamboo poles. A large collection of rifles filled a glass case to the right of the door and an impressive array of hand-guns filled an angled display case to my left. Books spilled over on side tables in the midst of which could be seen, fighting for space, an up to the minute computer and printer. Dominic's desk was exquisitely carved Malayan teak topped with a deep red leather inlay. It was large enough to accommodate the latest telephone equipment, answer phone and fax. A gold framed photograph of Susie smiled broadly at the observer next to which lay a carefully placed leather handled letter opener and matching inkpot. Six wire baskets of varying colours and brimming with papers lay in a neat row on the opposite side to the chair. A red leather antique chair had been neatly placed under the desk. Finally, in the centre of the large rectangular ink-pad lay Abdul's leather bound book. "Take a seat over here," said Dominic as he breezed into the room. I turned to see two comfortable leather armchairs placed in front of the open French windows. I've asked Mrs Lee to bring us coffee. You didn't eat much for breakfast, are you not hungry?"

"I'm absolutely fine thanks" I said, still feeling somewhat angry after the previous evening's argument. "Look Joanna, I'm sorry to have upset you last night but I really do feel that Laurent is up to no good." He said unexpectedly. "Let's face it, why should someone ten years your junior take a sudden interest in you unless he had an ulterior motive!"

My god, the nerve of the man, I slowly counted to three and threw my head back in a most defiant manner. "It seems to have escaped your notice Dominic that men of all ages do actually find me attractive!" I said scornfully. "Since you married your Malayan girl you have obviously lost the ability to recognise such things!"

"Coffee for two!" Announced the cheerful Mrs Lee. "And isn't it time the two of you stopped squabbling like children?" The door closed softly behind her leaving us sitting like children in detention after the senior mistress had left the room! Slowly and deliberately, Dominic reached for his coffee. He took a large mouthful and gazed out over the gardens to the lake. I waited for him to speak, rather than say something that I might regret and slowly sipped at my own coffee. A full two minutes passed before he stood and went over to his desk. He returned with Abdul's book and as if a little afraid of what he might find, tentatively lifted the well-worn cover.

"The 2nd February 1951." Dominic began. *"His Highness has tonight told me of his plans for the assassination and that I am to travel with him and Worme to Perai. My wife and children are under threat of death to prevent me from saying anything to anyone. I am afraid of what lies ahead of me and am fearful that my wife will be made a widow. If I do die then perhaps this diary will help those who wish to avenge my death."* Dominic raised his head and we exchanged a silent acknowledgement. He continued to read stopping only briefly to fetch more coffee. I watched his serious face and listened to his deep cosmopolitan voice, which remained low and surprisingly steady. Despite his apparent composure I was certain that the terrible crimes recorded in Abdul's book were having much the same effect on him as they were on me. By the time Dominic had turned the last page no less than seventeen assassinations had been carried out and numerous other murders! For several minutes we sat in silence. I felt sickened and deeply sad. I thought of my poor mother who had suffered the beatings and verbal abuse. I thought of myself the child, who had cowered behind

the beach hut when the shouting became intolerable. If only I had known the full story, I would never have allowed my father back into the house after my mother had died. I had actually felt sorry for him! "Dominic." I said urgently. "I must make contact with Abdul's wife, I have to ensure that she is going to be all right" "Joanna," Dominic replied firmly, "none of this has been your fault. You are not responsible for anything your father has done, you must come to terms with that fact." "How can I?" I found myself fighting back the tears. "I have to try and help those whose lives have been ruined by that unfeeling bastard. Perhaps, at least, I can make the Prince's last few days as miserable as possible!"

Dominic reached for my hands and pulled me to my feet. "Go out onto the balcony and I'll fetch you a nice bowl of fresh strawberries and cream. You hardly touched your breakfast."

Dominic's ability to swing from hostility to kindness continued to amaze me. He remembered my liking for strawberries and cream as if it was yesterday! I sat down on a comfortable cushioned rocking chair and let the perfume of the nearby herb garden fill my nostrils. It was a beautiful morning, the sun had risen quite high in the sky, which was a deep azure blue. Tiny fluffs of sharply contrasting white cloud hung as if suspended from invisible threads of cotton, and a gentle breeze was tickling the petals of a heavily blossomed Lotus tree. I stretched out in the rocking chair, kicked off my sandals and rested my heels on a low wooden table. Slowly I took in several deep breaths and felt my body begin to relax a little. Vaguely I heard the sound of an engine and then muted voices; someone had obviously arrived to see Dominic, as Susie had left early for university. Moments later, the sound of voices grew louder and were coming from the study.

"Joanna!" Dominic was already calling me as he rushed out on to the veranda. "My man is back with news of the Prince and the discovery of Abdul's body in his utility. The police arrived at the Prince's house just over an hour ago and have arrested his son Hussein. According to the house-keeper she discovered the body just after 9.30 this morning and immediately telephoned the police. It seems that the Prince has taken a turn for the worse and his personal physician is with him now."

"I want to see the Prince." I said without thinking. "Ask your man to take me to his house straight away!"

Dominic's jaw dropped. "For God's sake Joanna, pull yourself together. We were going to discuss our next move rationally or have you forgotten already?"

My mind was racing. I was torn between the need to gloat in the face of the man who had helped destroy my mother and to see him again simply to hold on to the last link with my former life. However, his son could not be to blame for his father's atrocious past, any more than I was responsible for my father's evil doings.

"We didn't reckon on his son being arrested" I gasped. "As much as this will bring grief to the Prince, we can't let his son take the blame!"

"Now this is where you could be completely wrong, Joanna." Dominic reached for my hand and once again gently pulled me up from my chair. "Come and meet my man, he'll fill you in on the son. I think you may think differently once you have heard what he has to say."

"Hussein is his father's son in more senses than one." Vic Amory lent across Dominic's desk and reached for the inkpot. He flipped the top and a flame shot out with which he lit a filter tipped cigarette. He was a big man, almost as tall as Dominic, fair thinning hair and pale blue twinkling eyes. He had probably been very attractive in his youth, but now carried the girth of a man who enjoyed more than a few beers each day and the deep furrowed brow of a man who spent a lot of time squinting in dimly lit bars. I learnt later that Vic had retired early from the Marines due to a mild heart condition. His estranged wife had committed suicide in the bath a few months later, after which he decided to return to the Far East. Vic, like Dominic, was a skilled armourer. He had at one stage been Dominic's sergeant and the two had become firm friends. Dominic was able to offer him a job as his right hand man and they had now been together for twelve years. "Although it has never been proved" Vic continued, "it is widely known that Hussein was heavily involved in the Communist Revolutionary effort in the late 70's. He was known to have recruited Malays and Chinese, to join up with the Insurgents and to wreak terror in the jungles using booby traps. The Prince secretly encouraged his son though was extremely careful to distance himself from the actual acts of violence. I would not be at all surprised if this latest atrocity with Abdul had something to do with Hussein!" "What about the Prince's gorilla?" I asked.

"Oh yes, our bald headed friend!" Dominic bent down and unzipped a large black tennis bag. Reaching inside, he found what he was looking for and threw it fiercely towards Vic. Vic's right hand moved like lightning and caught the tennis ball in his mighty grip. "When it comes to actually wielding the knife the Gorilla will almost certainly be our man." "So what do we do next?" I asked, trying to move things along as quickly as possible. "Vic is currently working as an 'investigative journalist' and will therefore be 'covering' the story. Any questions he asks will be assumed to be for a newspaper. In the meantime you and I have some strawberries and cream to eat!" Dominic laughed. The strawberries were delicious and I probably ate more than my fair share. Dominic, meanwhile, explained how he thought we could best make use of the information we had and how the current situation with Hussein's arrest could benefit us. Firstly, he would ring Max in Singapore. They were firm friends and Max was always keen to take any opportunity to come and stay at Dominic's place. Max, being Chief of Police in Singapore, would be able to obtain first-hand information from the Police headquarters in Kuala Lumpur. Vic, meanwhile, would be "on site" at the Prince's house watching all the comings and goings. Dominic felt that it would be safe for us to visit Abdul's wife as soon as his death was made public. Once the police had informed her of Abdul's murder she would almost certainly come straight to Kuala Lumpur. Dominic would also telephone Abdul's old friend, the Commander. He would definitely want to know about the tragic event and could, without doubt provide some support for Abdul's poor widow. Whilst all the organising was going on I went up to my room and lay down on the bed for a while. Deep down I felt a nervous sense of foreboding. I simply could not put my finger on what exactly was causing this, but one thing I did know was that I had to get to see the Prince. Dominic was totally against this, but nevertheless I felt compelled to get there somehow. "There's a couple of things I need to get in KL, can one of the men drive me in whilst you are organising things?" I smiled sweetly at Dominic, whom I had interrupted during a detailed discussion with two of his men. "All right Joanna" Dominic said unexpectedly "you can meet Max at the airport when you've finished, his plane arrives at six thirty. Jon will take you and stay with you whilst you are shopping, you can't be too careful in the current circumstances!"

The little Malayan called Jon, stepped forward and bowed. "Please to follow me Miss Wilde." Jon was a very cocky little fellow and chatted all the way into the city centre. We pulled into a multi-story carpark and then made our way on foot to a large department store. As soon as I had loaded Jon up with as many bags as he could carry I sent him back to the Jeep on the pretence that I needed to try on some underwear, and there was no sense in him waiting around in the lingerie department. He was most unhappy about this but reluctantly agreed to come back in fifteen minutes. As soon as Jon had disappeared out into the street, I rushed through a side entrance and hailed a rather battered looking taxi. The driver did not speak very good English but understood 'Prince Abdullah's House'. We crawled painstakingly through the city centre traffic and at last we were heading into the greener suburbs. The house was hidden from the road by a deep grove of coconut palms and the main gate was surrounded by reporters and cameramen. Two burly guards stood facing the crowd with their arms firmly folded.

As if by magic, the guards stepped backwards, opened the gates and waved the taxi through. I could not believe my luck, this had been as easy as pie - perhaps too easy! The passenger door beside me suddenly flew open and the heavy weight of a man leapt into the moving car beside me! His right hand reached inside his jacket and pulled out a revolver. "What the hell are you doing here, do you have a death wish?" Vic growled into my ear. "You had best be prepared for anything, do you have a gun?" "For god's sake Vic, you are taking this much too seriously." I gasped. "The Prince won't do me any harm, I just need to speak with him."

The car came to a sudden jerking halt outside the front entrance to the house. The passenger doors were pulled open and two doubled barrelled shotguns were thrust into our sides! "Throw the gun out English pig!" shouted a familiar voice. I peered out and upwards into the snarling face of the Gorilla and smiled sheepishly. "Oh, hello it's you!" I found myself saying in a rather silly sickly voice. "Please don't worry, my friend here was just trying to protect me, I've explained that you don't wish to harm me, so there's no need to take his gun."

"If Miss Wilde would be so kind as to come with me please." The Gorilla had immediately softened his tone and reached for my hand. His firm grip lifted me out of the car and onto the first step to the mansion house. The entrance porch was massive and framed by two immense stone pillars. The facade of the mansion appeared Victorian with deep sash windows stretching away from me on both sides of the black painted front door. The door's furniture was highly polished brass, which shone, menacingly in the afternoon sun. The darkness of the mansion's interior awaited me like the cavernous mouth of a hungry whale and I stepped gingerly forward in the wake of the retreating Gorilla.

"Why have you come now, do you wish to gloat?" The Prince could only manage a hoarse whisper. "I really am not quite sure, I just felt compelled to see you before you died. I assume you are close to death!" I said rather too casually. The Prince lay half propped up by large white lace trimmed feather pillows. His tiny grey face had sunk even further into deep hollows and the whites of his cold black eyes were red and watery. He held a portable oxygen mask in his right hand and his left hand rested on a copy of the Curran.

"You only told me half the story when you came to see me in Devon. You and my father did what you did purely for financial gain and to satisfy your lust for killing!" I blasted. "If your son is charged with murder you will not be able to escape your deserved punishment by dying. No, you had better stay alive to try and save his skin hadn't you!"

"You are no better than your father," the Prince wheezed. "Hussein is my only son, my only link with the memory of my beautiful wife. Your father took her away from me and now he is taking my son too." "It is no more than you deserve, evil begets evil" I smirked.

"Even if I wanted to, the cancer is too advanced for me to help Hussein. He is not guilty of murder, he was here with me yesterday; he never went to Malacca." The Prince sighed deeply.

"He didn't need to wield the knife to be guilty of murder" I stormed. "You can't deny that he has been doing your dirty work for years. We have clear evidence that you threatened Abdul and his family with murder on several occasions."

The Prince was making strange gurgling noises and he had suddenly gripped my hand, which felt as if it was in a steel vice. He was trying to speak but no sound came from his thin lipless mouth. I put my ear close to his face and through the deep gasps I heard, "Joanna, beware your father ...." An ominous rattling sound was coming from his chest and his eyes widened in horror. Like a stranded fish his skeletal body writhed in the bed gasping for air and spittle darted from the side of his blue lipped mouth. Then the Prince of darkness let out one last hissing breath and he was gone.

The large heavy hand on my shoulder, shook me gently back to reality. My hand was still in the Prince's death grip and with difficulty I prised his fingers away and released it. The Gorilla helped me gently to my feet and turned me towards the bedroom door. Vic stood waiting on the landing flanked by the two burly guards, he looked hugely relieved. I looked back through the doorway and saw the Gorilla slowly sink to his knees and take the Prince's hand in his. He bowed his head as the tears began to flow down his large round face. I quietly closed the door and in a daze headed for the stairs. Vic held onto my arm all the way back to the department store and into the lingerie department. Poor Jon was arguing with the floor manager and was insisting that he be allowed to check the changing rooms. The look of horror was unforgettable when he saw me arrive with Vic and he was not at all pleased when he realised how foolish he had been. We arrived at the airport with just minutes to spare and Vic rushed into the reception lounge to collect Max. "Well, well, we meet again Miss Wilde!" Max climbed into the back of the jeep alongside Vic. "It seems that you're coming to Malaysia has opened up a whole of cans of worms!" He laughed. "That's an old joke I am afraid." I said defensively. "Has Vic told you that the Prince is dead?"

"Yes he has, and it will be extremely interesting to hear the tape recording of the Prince's last words." Max grinned. "What tape recording?" I said, surprised. "The one in the bug you're wearing under your collar," laughed Vic. "I slipped it there before you got out of the taxi!"

Chapter 19

I had never been so humiliated in my life. It was like being a teenage girl in the pub and being forced to sit with the girls, whilst the boys all hogged the bar. Dominic and his cronies sat on the veranda drinking beer as if they had just returned from a visit to a local rugby match! I may as well have not existed until it came to a shortage of iced beer and wave of Dominic's arm in the direction of the kitchen. Determined to make my presence more than felt, I marched over to him with my hands firmly and aggressively placed on my hips! Max lifted his arms above his head in mock defence and wailed. "Please miss, it wasn't my idea, please don't use the cane......!"

"All right Max, leave her alone!" Dominic said, half-heartedly. "Look Joanna, I know your upset but it was your own fault for being so bloody devious. I thought you might try to slip away from Jon and quite naturally we took advantage of that fact. You have to admit that I was pretty resourceful and have a bloody good team around me!" "Well, you are right about one thing, I am upset and I have no intention of staying around to be laughed at by you or these idiots any longer. I'm packing and leaving! Please arrange for one of your men to drive me to the best hotel in KL in exactly one hour. Oh yes, last but not least you, Dominic, are sacked!"

You would have thought that I had just kicked a winning drop goal right into the open mouths of the spectators. I swept through the study and up to my room in no doubt whatsoever that I had made the right decision. Within minutes, a pale faced Susie was rushing through the door and pleading with me to stay. But absolutely nothing would persuade me to wait a moment longer. I agreed, however, to allow Susie enough time to arrange alternative accommodation and yes, if a room could not be made available before the morning then I would wait until then. But not a moment longer. Susie personally brought me dinner in my room and two large glasses of their best champagne. She was quite visibly shaken by my decision to leave and I actually began to feel a little guilty by the time she left. She explained to me that Dominic had, for years, spent too much time in the company of his male friends. As much as she loved him dearly, she did have her own younger friends and her Uni-life that took up a great deal of her time. She had hoped that some good would have come from my visit, particularly as Dominic was so fond of me! Susie was so very sweet, it had obviously never occurred to her that I could be a threat in any way, but then in reality there was probably no contest!

Dominic had gone out with the lads and Susie with her friends. The house seemed strangely empty with only Mrs Lee to talk to. I took my empty tray into the kitchen and thanked her genuinely for looking after me so well. Afterwards, I decided to go for a quick shower before an early night. Dominic's shower room was very male, with black tiling and stainless steel everywhere. I felt that I was somehow intruding and resolved to be in and out of the room as soon as possible. Back in my bedroom, I wrapped myself in a silk dressing gown, which had been thoughtfully left on the bed and opened the doors to the veranda. The night was a little cooler for a change and the huge moon hung in the sky like a heavy hazy doleful peach. I unwrapped my hair from the towel and shook my head over the edge of the balcony. I would leave it to dry naturally and relax on the bed for a while.

I could just make out the sound of the returning jeep and then the slurring of men's voices in the study below. Dominic and his cronies were back and still making a night of it. I quickly ran down the corridor to return the damp towel and placed it over the hot towel rail. My gasp of surprise was louder than I had realised on hearing the shower start! Dominic threw back the curtain and let out a loud drunken laugh!

"Well its Joanna 'haughty' Worme, she just couldn't resist one last look before disappearing out of my life again?" The naked Dominic lurched forward, the smell of whisky strong on his breath. I spun quickly towards the door and reached for the handle but Dominic was faster. With my wrist tightly clenched in his large hand he lifted me bodily into the shower cubicle and pinned me to the wall. The shock of cold tiles against my shoulder blades caused me to gasp and fall forwards. Dominic's dripping body forced me back, as his unshaven face leered into mine. The combination of aggression and passion as he kissed me, was completely overwhelming and I found myself just too shocked and weak to think of fighting him off.

When we were at last exhausted, Dominic released his once fevered hold and carried me out of the cubicle. Placing a large warm towel around me, he proceeded to gently rub me down. I simply could not hold back the tears of emotion, then as if woken from a dream he turned and left the room, closing the door to the bedroom firmly behind him! For a full minute, I stood in the middle of this black tiled emporium in a state of shock and disbelief. Would Dominic have raped me, if I had not responded positively?

"Joanna, I'm really sorry...I had no right...It probably is best that you leave." Dominic stood in the doorway wrapped in a towelling robe staring at the floor. "It was the drink...I can understand if you hate me....it probably makes us even anyway!"

I was astounded. "What on earth are you saying? I have never hated you, I could never understand why you didn't write to me, contact me....but I never hated you! There had to be a good reason for you to abandon me!"

"Abandon you! You're the one who didn't write, you're the one who killed our baby.... I've hated you for over 25 years....you nearly destroyed me!" He turned back into the bedroom, the big upright man now bent over with emotion as he dragged himself towards the balcony doors.

Now I understood the crushing hostility when we had first come face to face in Singapore and the deep seated anger raging inside him ever since. Dominic believed I had aborted our child, he knew nothing about Emma! I walked quickly across the bedroom and onto the balcony to see the man I still loved leaning heavily on the rail and staring out over the lake to some lost horizon.

"Dominic, listen to me, I did not kill our baby. You are the father of a beautiful daughter, her name is Emma!"

I watched and waited for what seemed to be an eternity. Dominic remained absolutely still, like a white marble statue, until at last he took a long slow deep breath and turned to face me. His face had taken on deep shadows in the moonlight and his eyes seemed to have darkened to the deepest of blue. I slowly walked over to him and took his hand. Silently we walked to his bed and sat down side by side. With his face in his hands, Dominic began to tell me his incredible story.

We had agreed that it would be best for him to write to my Father's house as I had been uncertain about the lease on my flat. Dominic had written as soon as he was allocated accommodation in Singapore. He wrote several times after that but received no reply. He became very worried at first, but concern turned to anger when, after the baby was due to be born he still had no communication from me. Three months later he had two weeks leave and flew to England. My Father had been extremely hostile and told Dominic that I had aborted the baby, married someone else and had left the country! Absolutely devastated, he returned to Singapore, vowing never to set foot in England again!

We held each other for a long time, silently but speaking volumes. The sound of a vehicle arriving finally shook us out of our cocoon and realising that Susie was home, I quickly kissed Dominic gently on the forehead and slipped out through the shower room, collecting the sodden silk dressing gown on the way. At some time during the night Dominic slid into the bed beside me. He held me gently for quite a while and then slipped away having persuaded me not to leave in the morning.

I woke the following morning feeling terribly confused. Dear sweet Susie was delighted that I was staying on, but I could not look her in the face, the situation seemed hopeless. Dominic was out on the estate when I arrived downstairs for breakfast, which further added to the crisis I now found myself having to deal with. Then to further add to my dilemma, Mrs Lee handed me a message from Laurent, which had been left on the answer phone at 7.30 the previous evening! I tried to concentrate on my reason for being there in the first place but this was proving more and more difficult. I headed for the study intending to re-read Abdul's diary and to formulate some sort of plan of action. I felt very close to Dominic in this room, surrounded by his personal collections and memorabilia. I sat in the armchair where I had listened to him reading and longed for a bowl of strawberries. I closed my eyes and drew in the warmth of the sun, which was pouring through the open French window, and my mind went back over the events of the last few days.

I had only left England five nights ago, yet it seemed like an eternity. I had been under surveillance from the moment I had left Devon leaving my darling daughter in potential danger. I had met Laurent whom I had totally trusted and could no longer be certain of. How had he obtained Dominic's number? I had met Abdul and learnt of the dreadful way he had been treated, only to find the wretched man's murdered body in the back of the jeep! I had witnessed the death of the Prince who in his dying breath had tried to warn me of something. What was he trying to say? I felt uncomfortable about Hussein being held in custody. But why? Surely, the events of the last few days could not simply be over the loss of a ruby and diamond necklace. It all seemed too incredible.

I sensed his presence and then the familiar smell of shower gel. His frame filled the open doorway of the French window and blotted out the sun. I felt the lump in my throat and then the nervous tightening in the stomach. "Good morning lovely lady, would you like strawberries with your coffee?" Dominic moved confidently from the veranda and placed his hands, one on each of the arms of my chair and kissed me gently on the forehead. I could not believe the overwhelming feeling of love I felt for this man, who had been hidden away in my memory for so long. I fought the urge to reach out for him and to take him into my arms, instead I looked down feigning coyness and said that I would love strawberries with my coffee. He flopped into the other armchair and let out a deep sigh. "Wow, I feel good. Don't you just think that the worlds a wonderful place Joanna?"

"To be honest, I'm very confused Dominic," I said carefully. "I really don't think I should stay here any longer, not after last night. What about Susie, have you given any thought to her reaction should she find out? I am so fond of her and she loves you so much!"

"I am going to tell her everything this evening and I want you to be there. I know she will understand, she's a great girl! She is very young and has her whole life ahead of her!" And, with that amazing statement, Dominic went off to order coffee and strawberries.

The next couple of hours were spent concentrating on our research, with the occasional smile and quick cuddle, simply because we could not entirely ignore our new situation. Dominic explained that Max had left early for police headquarters to see how the murder investigations were progressing. Vic was stationed outside the Princes house watching the comings and goings of the funeral preparations. Apparently, the Prince had a goddaughter who lived in a cottage in the grounds, so at least someone was in charge of the arrangements. The Commander was collecting Abdul's widow and they would be arriving by train around teatime that day.

Around eleven o'clock Dominic reached for a tiny tape cassette player and pressed play. I recognised the Princes voice immediately and then my own rather pompous outburst at his death bed. "....but he is not guilty of murder, he was here with me yesterday, he never went to Malacca." The Prince had said. Dominic played it back three more times "He never went to Malacca....".

This then proved that the Prince knew the murder had taken place and in Malacca, it still did not prove that his son had wielded the knife. I suggested that I pay another call on the Prince's house and to offer my condolences to his goddaughter. I would offer to assist with the funeral arrangements and, indeed, make myself as indispensable as possible. Dominic agreed to this on the basis that I should not come to any harm, based on my previous experiences. He insisted, however, that I keep a mobile phone with me at all times. After lunch he drove me into KL, stopping off on the way to buy a large bouquet of flowers. We arrived at the gates to the Prince's house and were waved through without challenge. The massive pillared frontage of the house once again came into view and a rush of apprehension surged into my chest. Dominic, on the other hand, looked extremely cool and collected. As I watched the jeep turn and disappear back down the gravelled drive, I felt extremely alone and vulnerable.

"You're Joanna Wilde aren't you?" The voice was female, cold and decidedly unwelcoming. I turned to find a tall, dark eyed, white woman in her mid-twenties standing in the doorway. Her short boyish hair was bleached blond and gelled flat against her small head emphasising the full red lips and long dark eyelashes. She wasn't pretty, but she was striking and the tight black leather trouser suit followed every contour of her slim but muscular body. "I suppose you had better come in!" I mumbled my thanks and followed her into the dimly lit entrance hall. The woman pulled on an embroidered bell rope and took the flowers from me. A maid appeared from behind the grand central staircase and was instructed to take the flowers and to bring coffee to the drawing room. I was led into the extremely grand drawing room. Several recognisable priceless paintings, or exceptionally good copies, adorned the oak panelled walls, gold leaf was on just about everything and the furniture was straight out of Buckingham Palace. The shutters were closed and the room was lit by hundreds of white candles that flickered and danced on the walls as we walked past. An immense portrait of the Prince, probably in his forties, dominated the room over the cold white marbled fireplace. The woman motioned me to sit and I selected a large cushioned armchair close to the unlit, but laid fireplace. The air was extremely cold but I could see or hear no sign of air-conditioning. The Amazon remained standing, her thumbs hooked into her front trouser pockets and her black booted feet set firmly apart. She stared intently towards the door and said nothing.

After a few minutes the silence became unbearable and I attempted to start a conversation but she raised her hand to silence me. "We will talk over coffee, I'll give the maid exactly one more minute, any longer and she's fired!" Thirty seconds later the maid scurried in struggling under the weight of an immense silver tray. She place it on a low lacquered table, then the nervous woman was immediately waved out of the room.

"My name is Cordelia, I hate the name...you may call me Cord. I am the Prince's goddaughter, although he treated me more like a daughter. I expect to benefit from the estate, but I don't care one way or another." This matter of fact information was imparted almost as a duty rather than a courtesy.

"I am sorry that we are meeting on such a sad occasion." I responded in as friendly a manner as possible. "I would like to offer my assistance and friendship during this difficult time..."

"You and I could never be friends, Joanna Wilde, I know all about you, I've known about you for years!" She turned and stared at me for the first time, her black eyes flashing in the candlelight. "Unfortunately the Prince made Hussein and I promise that you should come to no harm after his death. Hussein is innocent, you know. If you want to be of any real help you can use your influence and contacts to get him released!"

She curled her long red painted fingernails around her coffee cup and turned towards the painting. For a long time she stared intently into the Prince's stern face and at last relaxed her shoulders a little. I looked at her profile, her small nose and full lips sat oddly above the square set jaw. Her origin was hard to define and her accent was English with a slight American drawl. I seemed to be making little headway with this icy cold woman and racked my brains as to how to further the conversation.

"I agree that Hussein could not have killed Abdul and I will do my very best to get him released" I said as genuinely as possible. "Do you know where the Prince's bodyguard was over the two days before the body was found?"

Again, I had said the wrong thing. "You can forget about trying to pin this on Yeuw. In fact it will be in your interest not to ask any questions at all!" she hissed. A pregnant pause ensued. "Forgive me Cord, but I do not see how I can help Hussein without asking at least some questions. If we can establish who really wielded the knife then Hussein will be a free man," I offered.

Cord spun round spilling a small wave of coffee over the Turkish rug. Her eyes smouldered with hatred and I could feel the stabbing thrust of her venom in my throat. "You are a lying bitch, Joanna Wilde! How dare you come to this house and offer a hand of friendship. You tried to set the Prince up and instead put the finger of blame on Hussein. We don't need your kind of help, if I had my way I would strangle you with my bare hands here and now!"

"CORD!" The rather high pitched voice of command came from the far end of the room. We both turned to see a rather plump and much younger version of the Prince framed in the doorway. The man advanced towards us and with outstretched arms received the gushing Cord as she raced towards him. "Hussein, Hussein you have been released...but how?"

Hussein held the oddly emotional woman at arms-length and smiled. "I am released from custody, but we are all to be held under house arrest until after the funeral." He explained. "All, what do you mean by ALL?" Gasped the now incredulous Cord.

"By 'All', we mean every single person belonging to this household and includes staff living outside of the perimeter. They are being collected at this moment!" Max had quietly followed Hussein into the room. "I am afraid that this must also include you Miss Wilde, at least for the time being. We have reason to believe that you may have been the last person to have seen the murdered man alive."

Both Hussein and Cord turned towards me and slow smiles began to creep over their faces. I felt an innate sense of foreboding and lifted pleading hands towards Max. Max widened his eyes enough for me to receive a silent message of comfort, and addressed himself to the two officers at his side. He instructed them to arrange for all exits from the house and grounds to be manned, nobody was to leave before the funeral, which was arranged for two thirty the following day.

"I would like to make a private phone call." Max responded to my request by leading me by my elbow out of the drawing room and into a smaller anti-room. "Max, what on earth is going on?" I gasped, after he had closed the door behind him.

"Joanna, I am sorry to have put you in this position but I am afraid that I have no choice. A witness has come forward who claims to have seen Abdul leaving your hotel room in the early hours of the morning on the day he died." He sighed.

"But Max, you already know the whole story...you know I was not involved with the murder!" I gasped.

"Joanna, believe me, I am on your side and Dominic is one of my closest friends. The witness is on the murderer's payroll, you can be certain of that and you can be even more certain that we will get to the bottom of it. You're staying here will be very useful, and whilst Hussein and Cordelia believe that you are a potential murder suspect you will come to no harm." He put his arm around my shoulder and gave me a warm comforting smile. "By the way I hear you and Dominic are good friends again, I'm relieved to hear it."

Chapter 20

"Joanna?" Dominic's voice was audibly strained. "Before you say anything, Max has already phoned me. Are you OK, I mean really OK?"

"Yes, I'm fine" I lied. It was so good to hear his voice. After Max had left, a maid had shown me to a rather austere guest bedroom. The sudden switch in circumstances had struck an immediate change in Cords attitude towards me. She seemed to be relishing the idea of my having to stay at the house, where she could witness my discomfort and worry over what was to happen next. Hussein had taken an indifferent pompous attitude and preferred to avoid me. I gripped the mobile phone tightly and willed myself back into Dominic's large protective arms. "Are you still there Joanna?" I said that I was and Dominic filled me in with more detail surrounding the new "witness". She was an early morning cleaner at the club where we had stayed in Malacca. Worst of all she had also "seen" a heavy object being put into the back of the Jeep just before dawn. Subsequently, Dominic was also under house arrest! Despite his reassurances, I still felt a wave of panic take over after we had said our temporary goodbyes. The police guard could not be in every room of the house and as far as I could tell only the exit routes were formerly manned.

The funeral was to be a private affair due to the current police investigations. In normal circumstances a formal state funeral would have been arranged. According to the maid the Prince had not been particularly popular in KL, nor in Malaya itself. Despite this, a number of Sultans, other "Royals" and dignitaries, were expected at the house to pay their last respects in the morning. The body had been prepared and placed in its coffin in the Prince's private sitting room earlier that morning. Flowers continued to arrive and Cord seemed to be totally pre-occupied with the rushed arrangements. I had offered to help but was shooed away with an exaggerated wave of her hand. She had given the impression of someone hitting out at a strong smelling wasp!

I wandered down to the kitchens to find a hive of activity. Various carcasses were being dismembered and placed in baking trays. Piles of vegetables and fruit were being washed and sliced. The high pitched scream of the head chef's voice rang out at regular intervals over the hum of the constant chatter and I was relieved to see an open door to the garden a few yards away to my left.

"It is a little cooler. I think we will have a heavy shower soon." The uniformed police officer was short, but broad with more than his fair share of belly. "You are Miss Wilde." It was a statement not a question. No doubt the officers had been well briefed as to who was who. "You are free to walk around the gardens but please stay this side of the river," the Chinaman warned.

I was pleasantly surprised to find that the Prince had largely attempted to create the formality of an English country house garden. Tropical plants and trees mingled with young English oaks, Ash, poplars and boxed hedges. I wandered through an exquisite sunken garden with a twenty foot high fountain spouting from the raised jaws of a gigantic Chinese dragon. A rose garden carefully being tended by a coolie, hidden under a huge straw hat and finally to a fast moving tumbling river straddled by an immense red painted oriental bridge. I shaded my eyes against the blazing sun with my hand and slowly scanned the opposite river bank. Tall reeds grew in random clumps, whilst the grass was neatly mown for at least a hundred yards leading away from the bank, stopping abruptly at a line of natural jungle in the distance. How far the grounds stretched beyond those trees I could not tell. I continued to scan the river bank and was surprised to see a small single story cottage sitting alone with its own mooring and garden. The front veranda was in deep shade but I could just make out the wheels of a wheel chair glinting in the sun. I had been warned not to cross the river, which was most frustrating. My curiosity was about to get the better of me when I heard footsteps behind me.

I heard her laugh before I saw her. Yeuw, the gorilla, stood just behind her and bowed slightly in acknowledgement. "Looking for an escape route are we?" hissed the disagreeable Cord. She stepped forward until she was just inches from my face. "So typically English, red hair and freckles such a pity about the long scar across your right eye!" The sun glinted fiercely on the blade of a small ivory handled knife, which was being rolled through her red-taloned fingers. I winced and stepped back.

"No, Cord you are not to harm Miss Wilde, the Prince made you promise." The gorilla was gently but firmly holding her wrist. She wrenched it away and spat hard at my feet. "You must let the police deal with her, it will be all right." He prompted. For some reason this giant of a man had a calming effect and she turned and marched off towards the red bridge.

"Thank you Yeuw, I am grateful." I said genuinely.

"Do not thank me, I am only carrying out the Princes orders" he replied, obviously not wanting to be misunderstood. "I will stay with Prince Hussein, but I will miss my master, his death has put deep sadness in my heart." He stared across the river for a few seconds, turned and headed back towards the rose garden.

The sky had begun to darken and I too decided to return to the house. Before leaving, however, I shaded my eyes and watched Cord walk towards the cottage. She climbed onto the veranda and pushed the wheelchair, with its occupant, through an open door and closed it behind her.

By the time I got back to the house the rain was thundering down in stair rods. The air felt thick and humid as I watched huge puddles forming below my bedroom veranda. A knock at the door and the maid came in with a telephone and plugged it into a socket under the dressing table. "A Mr DuPont is on the phone and wishes to speak to you." She announced and left as quickly as she had arrived.

I gazed down at the receiver left off the hook and waiting to be answered. Laurent was ringing me here; how did he know? In slow motion I reached for the receiver and placed it to my ear.

"Joanna, ma petite angel, are you there?" I was completely dumb struck. I struggled with my reasoning but could find no answer. "Joanna, I know you are there. I have spoken to Mrs Lee who has told me what has happened. You are in grande trouble, that English pig has been the cause of this and I am flying to your side tonight!"

Somehow I found my voice, albeit a shaky one. "Please Laurent, I am perfectly all right. You do not need to come. Things have changed, I can't explain now, but please do not fly out to KL."

"Sacre bleau, Joanna, I love you! I will be with you in the morning and will not leave your side until I am convinced that you are safe." And he was gone.

As you can imagine, I spent a very restless night. Before retiring I had spoken with Dominic at some length on the mobile. I decided not to mention Cord's threatening behaviour or Laurent's telephone call, although I felt terribly guilty not telling him. We agreed to postpone breaking the news to Susie about our new found relationship and to concentrate on the problem at hand. I had also used the house phone to call Emma, which helped enormously. She enthused about the dogs, the garden, Harry, their wedding plans, Harry again, their long walks and visit to the beach, the dogs and Harry again. In between sentences, she castigated me for not ringing often enough and for the lack of postcards and, as usual, did not allow me breathing space to apologise or indeed to reply. Overall the one sided conversation did me an awful lot of good as did Harry's message that everything was still all right "in the garden."

I awoke at first light to the rattle of bone china teacups. The maid, who I had discovered was called Tam, apologised but the gentleman had insisted on bringing the tray himself. Laurent took the single red rose from the silver tray and placed it in my stiff sleepy hand.

"My darling, you look so edible with your tussled hair and sleepy eyes, I must make love to you straight away!" he whispered.

Tam had discreetly left, closing the door behind her. Suddenly I was wide awake and watching Laurent remove his shoes, shirt and now his trousers!

"No Laurent, wait!" I found myself throwing the bedclothes aside and rushing towards the bathroom.

"But you wish to clean your teeth, how very English and endearing," he laughed following me through the door.

"No, no Laurent, I can't do this .... Things have changed, I am in love with Dominic!" There was no easy way to tell him. I could not look him in the eye as I knew how this would hurt him. But, what was I thinking! In the heat of the moment, I had forgotten my reasons for mistrusting him!

Laurent had stopped in his tracks, his chin had dropped and for once he was speechless. I reached for a dressing gown and walked slowly back to the bedroom. The silver breakfast tray lay untouched at the bottom of the bed and the red rose lay dejected and forlorn on the pillow. I wrenched open the curtains then the French windows and another hot humid morning rolled in.

"I cannot believe that your love for me has simply died and so quickly. That Dominic has forced himself on you; that can be the only reason." Laurent stood beside me wrapped in his own arms as if to keep out some imaginary cold wind.

"I'm so sorry Laurent, I asked you not to come but you insisted and there is something that has been worrying me ever since I received your first phone call here in KL. Dominic insisted that there is no way you could have access to his private number, even his personal assistant is kept in ignorance. How did you really get hold of it?" I asked, still not looking at him.

Suddenly words of anger and frustration poured out of Laurent's mouth. "How dare you accuse me of not being honest with you, it is you who have been dishonest with me. That English pig will pay for what he has done!" He grabbed his shoes and jacket and stormed towards the door. Then as if suddenly realising what a spectacle he was making he turned and said, "I will book into the Hilton Hotel, when you come to your senses I will be there for you."

I felt overwhelmingly guilty, but Laurent had still not answered my question. He had flown to my side overnight and talked his way into a guarded house. It was all so confusing. Why would he go to so much trouble for a woman he did not love?

Not having any change of clothes, I climbed into yesterday's shirt and trousers. I found my way downstairs and followed the smell of cooking. A small but adequate breakfast table had been laid for six people and a cooked buffet, smelling quite delicious, awaited hungry tummies. It was interesting to note that the gorilla had a place at table. Hussein said very little and refused to look at me, whilst Cord filled me in on the details of the funeral. I was asked not to mention who I was, as there would be many who remembered George Worme and would not take kindly to finding his daughter in their midst. I was to say simply that I was an English writer and a friend of the family. The word friend did not roll easily off her tongue. I wondered whether Cord could possibly have any friends, if she did I could not imagine them being pleasant company on a dark night!

"You will need a change of clothes for the funeral service!" Hussein had broken his silence as I was taking my leave. "Tam will show you to my mother's dressing room, you are about her size...you are bound to find something to fit you."

In a state of surprise I followed Tam to the first floor and then to the west wing. This was the same route I had followed when visiting the Prince on his death bed. We passed the door to the Prince's suite and then turned sharp left into a bright upper hallway. I could immediately feel the strong female presence as Tam unlocked the door and led me into a dark but spacious sitting room. She carefully opened the curtains by pulling on two steel rods attached to top of each curtain that were at least fifteen feet high. As the light flooded in everything took on a rosy pink glow. The room was extremely feminine and rather Hollywood. The Princes late wife had, unfortunately, been greatly influenced by American movies of the fifties and early sixties. Everything was spotless, dust free and carefully preserved.

Tam had already moved on into an adjacent room and was again opening curtains when I joined her. More pinks and peaches dominated the room in the centre of which was a huge gilt bed sporting golden carved cupids on both the head and foot-boards. I suppose I could only describe the decor as pretty awful, but then that was only my humble English opinion.

Everything seemed frozen in time and I realised that I was probably seeing her rooms exactly as the Princess had left them, when she had run off with my father all those years ago! Tam's English was not particularly good but she was able to explain that the Prince had insisted on keeping the rooms exactly as they were. From the bedroom I was taken through a sliding door into a substantial walk in wardrobe....I felt my stomach lurch violently as I came face to face with the Princess! However, what I was really seeing was a mannequin wearing an early sixties summer dress, pinched at the waist with a full skirt over net petticoats. The dress was a deep petrol blue satin with a low neckline and small cup sleeves. The mannequin wore long white gloves, blue and white stiletto shoes and a matching broad brimmed hat. Audrey Hepburn would have died for this outfit! The whole length of the opposite wall was hung with exquisite designer outfits from smart tailored suits to the most dazzling of ball gowns. The sight of them took my breath away.

Tam excused herself and bowing low left the way we had come in. At the end of the dressing room, under the window, was an armchair and table and I was grateful for a moment's recovery. I sat and stared at the mannequin for quite a while and then my attention was caught by an array of photographs on the table beside me. Centre stage was a gilt framed picture of the Princess in a beautiful turquoise garden party outfit. She was very beautiful, blond and had an uncanny resemblance to my own mother! She was flanked on one side by the young Prince, who was at least six inches shorter and on the other by a British army officer. I peered closely at the smiling face of the officer and found myself staring into the dark eyes of my Father!

I felt desperate for Dominic's company, walked back into the bedroom and opened the window. Although the air was hot and humid, I was grateful to be out of the claustrophobic atmosphere of the dressing room. The sound of chattering voices drifted up from the garden and I could see awnings hastily being erected on the steaming lawns. Gritting my teeth, I went back to the wardrobe a started to look through the darker outfits. I found a black fitted crepe dress and matching short sleeved jacket, trimmed with dainty pearls and tried it on. It was a perfect fit. Black stilettos and little box hat with netting to cover the face set it off rather well. Feeling in need of a shower, I laid the outfit on the bed along with suitable matching underwear and stockings.

I must say that the pink marbled bathroom was lovely and in a rather macabre way I actually enjoyed showering and powdering myself with the rose perfumed talc. After drying my hair I felt it would look better tied up, if I was going to wear the box hat. I found suitable pins and clips in a little dressing table drawer and proceeded to twirl my now sun-bleached auburn hair up into a suitable twirl. Dressed in the whole outfit and satisfied with my final image in the long gilt mirror, I tidied up my belongings, closed the bedroom door behind me and entered the sitting room.

Hussein stood staring out of the window with his hands clasped firmly behind him. He turned slowly towards me as I entered the room and the sight of me obviously had quite a profound effect for the colour visibly drained from his face.

"My God," he gasped "you look the spitting image of my mother!"

"Actually our mothers had quite a close resemblance." I replied. "I was amazed when I saw the picture of the Princess in the dressing room."

Hussein stared into my eyes. This was the first real communication we had since his unexpected return the previous afternoon. He turned and stared out of the window, clasping his hands behind his back again.

"This is the first time I have entered my mother's suite, since her death. My father kept the door locked, only allowing the maid to enter once a week to keep it clean.

He was obsessed with her and your father. I wasn't sure which one had the most effect on him." He began to slowly circle the room running, his right hand along the top of the furniture as if he wanted to be sure it was all real. "I was still a boy when she died, my father sent me to England to be educated and then I returned to help fight the capitalist enemy. But that is all in the past now and since the mid-eighties I have concentrated on running my father's business and investment interests. You might be interested to know that I don't even own a firearm."

"Why are you telling me all this Hussein, you have every reason to distrust me in the current circumstances." I asked feeling rather perplexed at this impromptu flow of information.

"When my father told me he was travelling to England on a quest to find you, I felt certain there was a greater reason than this ruby and diamond necklace he had talked about. He had been given only weeks to live and I feared that he would die before managing to return home. I could not dissuade him and he set off with just Yeuw to escort him. When he returned he was almost euphoric, as if he could now at last die in peace." Hussein's brow was heavily furrowed as he turned back to look at me. "Can you shine any light on why he came to see you Joanna?"

He had used my Christian name and I felt, for the first time, a genuine sense of friendliness in his manner. Of course, I was no more enlightened than he was and said so, but our discussion made me even more determined to track down my father's movements after the Princess had died, leading to his own death just a few years later.

Chapter 21

I returned to my room with my things and then decided to go to the Prince's private sitting room to pay my respects before the official mourners arrived. His tiny skeletal face was very peaceful. The room smelt of incense and fresh flowers. The floor and every possible surface were swamped with flowers and wreaths. I looked back at the Prince and felt strangely emotional. He lay as if asleep, his head resting on an ivory silk pillow. He was dressed head to toe in gold embroidered silken robes, his tiny hands laden with oversized heavily jewelled rings. The cancer had probably caused the terrible loss of weight and I tried to imagine him as the once healthy man in the drawing room painting. Hussein was a fatter mirror image of that painting. His father would have been considered a handsome man. I tried to imagine my own father and the Prince together as friends; I still found this extremely difficult to do. Now they would be together again and almost certainly in hell if there was one!

The silence was broken by a muffled sound coming from a closed door next to an ornate bookcase. I put my ear to the door and listened carefully. I could just make out a groan and then gasps. Curious, I gently turned the ivory door-knob and opened the door just a crack. The sound of moaning and heavy breathing was suddenly increased by several decibels and to my horror, I found myself witnessing the most disgusting spectacle. Cord, naked from the waist down, was riding an equally half naked sweating gorilla on top of a snooker table. I hastily closed the door and spun round.

"Are you all right Miss Wilde?" The uniformed police officer looked concerned. "I have been sent to find Miss Cord, the first of the mourners are arriving."

"You'll find her through there" I smiled pointing towards the closed door. "Don't bother to knock."

I watched as the officer marched straight into the room, smiled sweetly at the Prince and left through the opposite door.

Ten minutes later Hussein and a flustered Cord were greeting the first arrivals in the great hallway. All kinds of nationalities were represented as they filed through to the Prince's sitting room and then into the candlelit drawing room for liquid refreshment. The furniture had been re-arranged to provide seating for the mourners during the hastily organised funeral ceremony. After the ceremony, only close family would travel with the body to the central mosque for burial and under heavy police guard.

For the benefit of the mixed races, prayers were said in several languages and finally the small funeral procession left the house disappearing slowly down the gravel drive and out towards the centre of KL. As I watched, I remembered that strange feeling of loss I had felt back at my Devon farmhouse, when the Prince had finally taken his leave. I had not expected to see him again. At that moment, I would have given anything to have been back at my garden gate with Dippy's warm black body pressed close to my bare leg. I longed to be able to walk to the top of Visitors Hill and to gaze out over those wonderful green and brown patchwork hills.

A comforting arm had been placed around my shoulders and was steering me back towards the house. Vic, wearing his press pass, had been granted access to the garden and house during this important occasion.

"Less of the long face, Joanna, things are moving along nicely on the home front." He whispered, whilst smiling and acknowledging passing mourners. "Dominic was contacted by Interpol last night and two guys arrived at his house this morning. It seems that there is a much bigger fish to fry than Hussein. I'll keep you posted." Vic moved off smoothly and began chatting with a group of Europeans.

Everyone, other than a few early leavers were wending their way back through the house and into the rear gardens. That morning, busy workers had finished erecting the cream canvas awnings under which directors chairs and trestle tables had been placed. Already waiters were serving drinks and passing around hors d'oeuvres by the time I had wandered out. I gazed out over this elegant scene and realised my extreme isolation despite the comforting distant presence of Vic. Then, as if my thoughts had been read, I discovered that I was far from alone.

"A glass of champagne for the beautiful lady?" The tanned perfectly manicured hand around the proffered glass, was immediately recognisable. Laurent flashed a white pleading smile and gently steered me towards a shady table. "Please do not send me away Joanna, I really must speak to you."

"How on earth have you managed to get past the police cordon?" I asked, genuinely amazed. "But I am your fiancée Joanna and it is important that you have your supply of insulin - well that is what I have told them - I would say anything to be with you Joanna, you must know that." Laurent looked terribly strained and for a fleeting moment had lost his usual air of confidence. It was easy to forget that I had every reason to distrust him, there was too much evidence to support it, and yet there was something about him, apart from the obvious physical attraction there was something that persuaded me to confide in him.

I told him everything, as mad as this sounds, I felt almost compelled to do so. He listened intently and at some stage had placed his hand on mine. A second glass of champagne appeared and at last I had completed my story. Now Laurent fully understood my feelings for Dominic and promised not to be a bad loser. He was charming and though obviously sad, would fly back to Singapore that night. I felt a mixture of sadness and relief as I watched him walk quickly towards the house and into the dark shade of the covered veranda. In another life, things might have been very different.

I felt an urgent need to speak to Dominic and reached into the Princess's handbag for the mobile. One of the guys from Interpol was still with Dominic and it appeared that during our innocent research into my father's last years, we had interfered with weeks of planning and the imminent arrest of an international criminal. He was unable to tell me anything else at this stage but assured me that we were in no danger of being accused of Abdul's murder. Abdul's wife had formerly identified the body and the Commander was arranging to have it taken back to Malacca for burial after the autopsy. In the meantime, he was taking responsibility for Abdul's wife's welfare and had booked them both into the Hilton.

For the next half an hour or so I was drawn into conversation with the British Ambassador and his wife and then stayed with them over a lavish banquet held in the Prince's opulent dining room. No expense had been spared, and the occasion would be best described as a celebration of the life of the Prince and gluttony. But all this time I felt on edge, the threatening stance of Cord every time she caught my eye and the discreet presence of uniformed officers.

Late afternoon and the sky had darkened yet again. The rain thundered down and quickly turned the garden back into the swamp conditions of the earlier evening. Frustrated mourners waited for their cars to arrive and slowly but surely thinned out to a few stragglers. After the last of the mourners had left, I returned the black suit to the Princess's bedroom and changed back into my casual clothes. The caterers were packing up and by 7 O'clock all that was left in evidence were the abundance of flowers and wreaths still to be transported to the mosque.

"For god's sake, I don't care how you get them there, I can't stand the smell any longer. If necessary put them on the bloody compost heap or burn them!" Cord was shouting angrily at an estate worker who had obviously been given the task of transporting the hundreds of floral tributes. Shaking with fear he was attempting to carry far too many bouquets and was dropping more than he was managing to safely take to an awaiting truck.

"Here let me help you," I said without thinking and began to assist the poor Chinaman who must have been at least seventy.

"That's about all your fit for....a skivvy," Cord spat at the ground and stormed off. We were joined by two other coolies and after half an hours hard work had loaded all the tributes very carefully into the open topped truck.

"You are pathetic, a wimp." Cord hissed from her vantage point on the dining room balcony. She had lit a small cigar and had perched herself on the balustrade. For the funeral she had donned a long black dress and veil but was now back into black leather trousers. "If George had known what a weak creature he had produced, he would have had you put down at birth." She was enjoying herself, taking great pleasure in the verbal diarrhoea she was spouting. If she could not hurt me physically then she would do it verbally. I had known this woman for less than twenty four hours, but she was easy to hate and hate her I did. She wanted to goad me into retaliation, but I was determined to bite my tongue. I would bring the bitch down somehow, but not this way.

The humidity of the early evening, along with the wine and food had left me exhausted. I dragged myself up the central staircase and back to my guest room. Throwing off my clothes, I collapsed naked under a single sheet and slept immediately. Down in the depth of the deepest of sleeps, I was fighting to find the ringing mobile. It was pitch black and the sound was terribly muffled. I threw back the sheet and fumbled for the bedside lamp only to knock it flying, but lit, onto the floor. The Princess's handbag lay half open on the dressing table and I staggered towards it. Damn! The ringing stopped before I could retrieve the phone. I looked at my watch, it was eleven thirty - I had slept for three hours!

Needing a wee, I headed for the bathroom clutching the phone and no sooner had I sat down when it started to ring again. "Joanna? Where were you, you're supposed to keep the phone with you at all times - we did discuss this, are you all right?" Dominic sounded angry but concerned. I was so relieved to hear his voice and felt wrapped in a warm blanket.

"I'm so sorry Dominic, I was exhausted and fell asleep." I replied in my softest voice. His voice immediately softened in response. "I miss you terribly Joanna, I wish to god they would lift this house arrest business. I have one of the Interpol guys staying here, it's a bit difficult to get any information out of him though. Max says they are following a new route of enquiry, which should put us in the clear very shortly. He would like you do a little bit of sniffing around though and tonight could be perfect timing. Hussein has a lady friend visiting and both Cord and the gorilla are being questioned down at police headquarters."

"What sort of sniffing around does he have in mind?" I asked, trying not to sound too apprehensive.

"You could start with the Prince's study and sitting room. Any evidence of recent illegal activity would do very nicely. You might also be able to find more information about your father's activities between running off with the Princess and his untimely death." Dominic said encouragingly.

I needed no other incentive. "I love you Dominic," I whispered. "I love you too, darling - take care, keep the phone with you." And he was gone.

My bottom had stuck to the loo seat in the heat. Prising myself carefully off, I reached for the shower tap and switched it on. Refreshed, wide awake and dressed in borrowed slacks and shirt, I slipped quietly out of my room into the dimly lit upper hallway. At the far end of the landing, a light shone under Hussein's door and the faint sound of female laughter gave me the comfort of knowing that he was well and truly occupied. Reaching the bottom of the central staircase I stood and listened. The sound of activity could be heard coming from the domestic quarters otherwise all was quiet. I quickly padded my way to the Prince's study and turned the doorknob. The door would not budge, obviously locked. I cursed silently under my breath and moved on towards the sitting room door. It opened! I closed the door behind me and switched on the light. The furniture and been re-arranged probably back to the way it was before the Prince had died. It was a comfortable room with two high backed armchairs and decorated to reflect the Princes taste for both English and Eastern culture. It was an uncluttered room, a room for relaxation and for entertaining a private visitor or two. I tried the opposite door to the one I had entered by, it opened and I stepped into the snooker room. I shuddered at the memory of Cord and the Gorilla and pressed the dimmer switch just inside the door. Intimate lighting flooded the room, the walls of which were hung with rich vibrant tapestries. A second dimmer switch lit the central lights over the snooker table. There was an incredible atmosphere in this room and I could imagine cigar smoking, brandy drinking royalty indulging in late night challenges. I let my eyes wander slowly around the room drinking in the rich hangings until I caught site of a smaller tapestry hanging from a hinged brass rail. I walked over and carefully pulled it towards me - it concealed another door!

The door was unlocked and I very gingerly opened it just a crack. It was completely dark in the room on the other side, so I had no choice but to enter it and feel for a light switch. The switch lit a lamp positioned on the edge of a massive ornate desk - I was in the Prince's study! Whoever had locked the outer door had completely overlooked this inner one. Three walls were lined floor to ceiling with bookshelves. In front of the shuttered French window was a single armchair and occasional table. Someone had already made considerable in-roads into sorting out the Prince's paperwork as a number of boxes and files lay on the floor under the table. Paper was also strewn over the table and desk and a large black dustbin bag was half full. This made things somewhat easier for me as the room was already in a state of disarray. My only problem was where to start!

The first thing to attract my attention was a small leather suitcase. Rather worn but looking particularly inviting. I lifted it onto the desk and tried the two clasps. It was locked. I opened the top drawer of the desk and found a collection of keys. One of the small silver keys fitted perfectly and I heard the lock spring open with rather a startling click. I held my breath and listened for several minutes before opening the lid. The case was full of letters some of which were carefully bound into separate piles. There were letters from all over the world and in particular, a bundle tied with pink ribbon from England. Just as I was attempting to look closer at the date of the top letter the phone on the desk started to ring! I nearly jumped out of my skin and only just managed to prevent the case from flying onto the floor. I quickly closed the lid and with it tucked under my arm raced silently through the concealed entrance switching off the light before closing the door behind me. I ran across the snooker room turning the dimmer switches off and pulled the connecting door to the sitting room shut behind me. By this time my heart was thumping so loudly I was sure it would wake the whole household. Sweat was pouring down my face as I reached for the sitting room light switch at last bathing myself in the comfort of darkness. Clutching the leather suitcase to my chest, I sat down in one of the high backed armchairs and waited. I listened hard trying to calm my breathing. The phone had been answered, as it was no longer ringing. I could not hear a voice coming from the study so the call must have been taken elsewhere in the house. I took in a silent deep breath and exhaled slowly. Then I waited until I was convinced that the house was silent and asleep.

Back in the relative safety of my room and with the door securely locked, I opened the suitcase. I spread the bundles of letters over the bed finally arranging them in date order. The earliest bundle (with the pink bow) was postmarked 1950. I sat cross-legged in the middle of the bed and stared at what could be a minefield of information. The pink ribbon bundle had to be love letters, some of the others also looked as if they had been addressed in a female hand. Then another bundle in a strong hand and all addressed in capital letters. The majority were postmarked as having been sent from England!

It was then that I realised I was getting a migraine - I had not had one for years. Sickness and nausea had started to well up through my stomach, throat and the pressure in my head was becoming unbearable. I lay my head back on my pillow knowing that the only way to relieve it was to close my eyes and rest. My vision had rapidly blurred and there was no chance of my reading anything for half an hour or so. Oh god, how I needed Dominic's strong arms around me at that moment. I reached for the mobile.

Where was the mobile? My impaired vision was preventing me from focusing properly. I concentrated hard but could not see it. I began to get angry with myself and despite the pain in my head, swung my legs over the edge of the bed and stood up. Then it hit me. The last time I had seen it was when I had put it down on the Prince's desk in his study. Oh god, how could I be so stupid! I felt my way along the wall to the door, into the upper hallway and half slid down the central staircase. A massive wave of nausea came over me as I steadied myself against bottom hand-rail.

Suddenly the hallway was flooded with light and the massive front door slammed shut with a great rush of wind.

"Look at the bitch, she's drunk as a skunk!" Cord's blurred face swam into vision. "Your daddy was a drunk, did you know that bitch .....?"

Unable to think straight or defend myself I sank down onto the bottom stair and closed my eyes. Then I heard it, the mobile was ringing!

"I can hear a phone ringing in the study, shall I answer it?" It was the gorilla's voice.

"Sure, go get it stallion," Cord laughed "I'll get the drunken bitch into the drawing room. I think we might have a bit of fun with this one."

I attempted to pull myself back up onto my feet and failed miserably. Cord squealed with laughter and caught me under my armpits. "Poor little bitch is pissed, poor little bitch is pissed!" she sang as she dragged me into the drawing room.

I managed at last to find my voice. "I'm not drunk." I gasped. "I'm having a migraine attack. I was on the way to the kitchen to find some painkillers."

Cord screamed even louder with laughter. "Your Daddy was also a brilliant liar, did you know that bitch?" She was poking me hard in the chest with her finger and I could smell whisky on her breath.

"The door to the study was locked." The gorilla had joined us. "The phone has stopped ringing now."

"Pour three large whiskies, let's have a party!" Cord's face was suddenly just inches away from my own and the cold sting of glass hit my teeth and gums. The whisky stung the back of my throat and I gulped and coughed in shocked reaction. Now she was thrusting the bottle into my mouth and was holding my nose. I tried to struggle out of my chair but her high-heeled boot was pressed firmly into my chest. The pain in my head intensified and at last the bottle was withdrawn from my mouth. Again, I tried to get up, but she was tying my wrists to the heavy chair - surely someone would hear the noise. My eyes had started to re-focus and to my utmost horror, I realised that the two lovers were thrashing away on the carpet at my feet. I closed my eyes tightly and felt the nausea rush up into my throat. Then I vomited, I felt as if the whole of my insides were being ripped out and then mercifully I slipped into blackness.

Chapter 22

Something damp and cool was smoothing my brow and I was lying on my back with my head resting on a soft pillow. I could hear voices faintly, but clearly, in the room and my head felt like lead. A bright light was trying to pierce my closed eyelids and with enormous effort, I finally managed to prise them open.

"Joanna, can you hear me?" Max swam into my vision. "She's waking up with a massive hangover Dominic. Yes, she'll be fine now she's all tucked up in bed. Yes, I'll make sure someone stays with her. Calm down man, just give us a little more time and everything will be sorted."

"Please, I want to speak to Dominic." My voice came out as a croak; I was desperate for a drink of water. "It was Cord, she forced me to down a bottle of scotch - the woman is a complete psychopath!" I gasped into the mouthpiece.

"Right, that's it. You are not to leave your room and Max must have a guard put outside your door. Promise me Joanna that you will not expose yourself to any more danger." Dominic's love and real concern echoed through the mobile and I promised that I would do exactly as he wished. I loved him too much to cause any further anguish.

Dominic asked to speak to Max again and at last seemed satisfied. He had telephoned Max after several failed efforts to contact me on the mobile. Max immediately alerted the outside police guard who had found me slumped in the drawing room clutching an empty bottle of Jameson. Max had arrived within minutes and had carried me back upstairs to my room. The maid had cleaned me up and put me into a night gown. I had apparently mumbled over and over again, about the mobile and the study. Max had managed to retrieve the offending article without disturbing the rest of the house.

I drank a long cool glass of water and rested my still aching head back on the pillow. When I next awoke it was very quiet and the moon was sending a slim shaft of light through the almost closed curtains. My eyes ached, but my head was no longer hurting and my vision had cleared. I slowly pulled myself up into a half sitting position and reached for the glass of water. I rested back against the pillows and went over the events of the previous few hours in my mind. I felt very angry. I was normally, in most senses of the word, a strong character but I had been made to seem weak and vulnerable in the eyes of everyone around me. I was determined to take my revenge on Cord, but in no way would I lower myself to her standards. I took my glass of water out onto the balcony and gazed out over the moonlit gardens. In the far distance, a dim light could be seen indicating the precise position of the cottage on the opposite side of the river, Cord's lair. Suddenly a brilliant idea hit me and I rushed back into the room to find my clothes! There was just enough light to see without switching on the lamp. My clothes had been neatly folded over a chair but as I reached for them I found myself falling over a hard object on the floor. The leather suitcase! In my excitement I had forgotten all about it. Placing it on the bed, I opened the clasps, being careful to prevent the springs from making any noise. The letters had been carefully replaced, thank heavens, whoever had done this had not realised the importance of their contents. I decided to postpone my brilliant idea as I could not resist untying the pink ribbon and opening the first envelope. I switched on the bedside lamp. The handwriting on the envelope was vaguely familiar, I looked at the postmark; it was dated 2nd January 1950 and had been posted in England. I took a very deep breath and eased the letter out of the envelope. As with any potentially good read, I was sorely tempted to read the senders name before I had read the letter. There were three pages written in pretty female handwriting on pale blue paper - I forced myself to start reading from the beginning.

"My Dearest Abdullah" it began, "I was so pleased to receive your letter and to have an address to correspond to. I too felt that our friendship had deepened by the time you returned home and have found myself thinking of you every day. I have taken temporary employment with the Post Office as a *telephonist at the Exeter telephone exchange and am working with a lovely group of girls who are all between the ages of 18 and 25. I am the only one to have attended university and my first class degree is considered rather amusing amongst my colleagues. I fear that I may have to leave my beloved Devon if I am to pursue a career in history or the arts. However, a possible teaching position may be available in September at Maynards (my old school).*

I continue to meet with most of our old friends, we are all struggling to find suitable postings. Your old room-mate, Tommy, is going for an interview with Cardiff University next week, we are all rooting for him. He sends his regards"

The letter continued with newsy items about other friends and then in the last paragraph she had written - *"We see George quite often, he is much quieter than he used to be. He always asks after you and I have promised to let him know if I hear from you. Is it all right to pass your address to him?"* And finally, the letter was not unexpectedly signed *"With great affection, Monique."*

I knew in my heart, after reading the first few lines that the writer was my mother. There were a further 14 letters and I felt compelled to read on. I began to feel and touch this young woman who was to become my mother. Her naivety, her love of the arts, books and poetry. Her fascination with Abdullah's world, and his country and her growing love for the Prince. But in letter twelve, I could feel things going terribly wrong, George was being mentioned more and more frequently. She seemed to have been encouraged by him to talk about the Prince's letters; he had become a sort of confidant in this respect. He had also been corresponding with the Prince, expressing his views on what he felt was best for Monique.

Then I opened letter thirteen and it read, *"My Dear Sweet Abdullah that you should ask me to be your wife is beyond my wildest dreams. To join you in Malaya is such an exciting prospect and I am so very flattered. But, my dear, you are a Royal Prince and I am a simple (if educated) Devon maid. George believes that it would be a terrible mistake and that you should be looking to marry a*

Princess or the equivalent. He is also a very good friend and he feels strongly that I would be very unhappy in your country with its strange customs and way of life. I fear that he could right but I do wish to think this over carefully before I make a final decision."

Monique's final letter had obviously followed one from Abdullah, which had pleaded with her to accept his proposal, he had also written a strong letter to George.

"My Dear Abdullah, I am deeply saddened by your last letter. George has been a very good friend over the last few months and I cannot believe that you could write to him in this way. He has never once tried to take advantage of me and your insinuation that he wants me for himself is completely unfounded." And the letter ended, *"My decision not to marry you is my final one. I do hope that you can find room in your heart to remain my friend and George's too. You will always remain in mine."*

George through evil selfish manipulation had broken two hearts. I could visualise Monique in George's arms, being consoled and slowly but surely being taken advantage of. The last letter was dated September 1950. I was born in June 1951.

My heart ached for my mother, her future could have been so different. If she had married the Prince the following 20 years might have been free from the murderous activities of George Worme. Another bundle of letters from George confirmed his and the Prince's continued friendship. George had told the Prince that he was marrying Monique because she had been raped by a local fisherman and was pregnant! The Prince had obviously been drawn into the belief that George was acting in Monique's best interest and thus the bizarre relationship between the two men had begun. A number of other unbundled letters were strewn randomly over the bottom of the case. I collected them together and placed them in date order, all were dated considerably later than the bundled ones.

There were very sweet love letters from the future Princess, correspondence from his mother who had obviously retired to Switzerland, and two letters sent from Singapore in 1982.

Having laid to rest the period leading up to the start of the Prince/Worme partnership I was not expecting to be presented with vital information on the period following the time my father had run off with the Princess! The two 1982 letters had been sent to the Prince by The Mother Superior, St Benedict's Priory Orphanage. To my utter amazement the first letter read as follows:

"Your Highness, It is under some considerable pressure from the Sisters and our serious concern over the mental health of one of our children that we write to you today. I do hope that you will understand that I am breaking a confidence only in the interest of the child and the future state of mind of the other children in our care. I know this will come as rather a shock and I apologise for the anguish this letter may bring you.

In late 1969 a young lady and her escort came to us for help. She was heavily pregnant and in need of sanctuary and protection during the birth of her child. This young lady was your wife, the Princess. She was accompanied by a Mr George Worme, who was most anxious about the sensitivity of the situation. Mr Worme arranged for a substantial amount of money to be held on account for us, to cover all our expenses and promised to return in two weeks' time. Five days later the Princess gave birth to a daughter, the baby was strong and healthy but the Princess died an hour later. We did everything we could to save her but to no avail. When Mr Worme returned he was devastated. After a further two days, he arranged for the body to be returned to you.

The baby was named Cordelia, has grown up here in the orphanage and is now 13 years of age. Mr Worme left further substantial funds for her upkeep along with a rather pretty charm bracelet, which had apparently belonged to his mother.

The last year has been extremely difficult, Cordelia has become very destructive and a bully. We have tried everything to calm her including medication but she continues with her violent outbursts. We are convinced that she needs a home and family, we have not heard from Mr Worme since her birth and are forced to look to you for help."

I put the letter down and taking a deep breath rested back on the pillow. The palms of my hands were sweating and my heart was thumping fast. Cord was my half-sister! Unless by some remote chance the Prince was her natural father, which I doubted, she was my bloody sister! This was utterly horrible, did she know, is that why she had treated me so badly? I grabbed the second letter and tore it open. The Prince had obviously responded instantly and was arranging to visit the orphanage a week later. The Mother superior had mentioned that Cordelia had a close friend called Yeuw, who she refused to be separated from. So, the gorilla makes his entrance!

I badly needed to talk to Dominic, but the bedside clock said 03.15 am. I rang his mobile anyway only to get his voice mail. I just left an "I love you" message and turned my thoughts back to the brilliant idea I had had earlier whilst looking out over the garden. Opening the bedroom door I peered out into the gloom to see a police guard positioned immediately opposite my room, half slumped in a large armchair. I cleared my throat, he stirred, sprung to his feet and stared, glazed with sleep, at me in my night gown.

"Miss Wilde! Is everything all right?" he whispered. "Yes, yes I'm fine" I smiled. "Where is Cordelia, did she return to her cottage?"

"The party ended about an hour ago and she went with Mr Yeuw to his room. You are quite safe Miss Wilde, there is a Guard watching his room as well." I thanked him, stepped back into my room and closed the door with a satisfied smile on my face. Great! I would put my plan into action immediately.

Chapter 23

I dropped very lightly from my bedroom balcony onto the soft damp grass below. Keeping low, I ran carefully from shadow to shadow through the rose garden to the river bank. The river was once more in spate and small waves of muddy water sloshed across the flattened grass towards me. Pieces of debris, including quite a substantial tree trunk, had been washed up onto the bank and that odd smell of previously undisturbed sub-soil filled my nostrils. Rain clouds continued to scud across the moon throwing everything in and out of darkness. The ornate carved wooden bridge seemed much bigger now that I was standing beside it, and I realised that I would easily be seen from the cottage as I crossed it. It was made of sturdy stuff, built to withstand the heavy volume of river water that probably rose considerably higher at the height of the monsoon.

I crouched and waited for the next rush of darkness then ran for the bridge. Despite my careful light-footedness, my feet made an unexpected dull thumping sound. On reaching the other side, I crouched low and waited awhile, getting my breath back. My heart was thumping like a steam train. The cottage showed no signs of life; the light I had seen earlier had been extinguished. The tall rushes growing this side of the river would help to conceal my approach from the main house and garden. Having got this far there was no way that I could go back. I made a dash for the side of the cottage, then tiptoed up the wooden steps onto the veranda where I had glimpsed the wheelchair the previous day. The river rushed six feet below hitting the support beams with a great roar and sucking sound. Any noise I might make would be easily drowned out. The French doors were open, but a sliding rigid framed mosquito net barred my way. It moved easily on its runners, so I stepped silently through carefully closing it behind me.

I stood for a few seconds and listened, nothing. The smell of cigarettes hung heavily in the room and the sickening smell of stale whisky wafted over from a cluttered sideboard. I could make out three doors leading off this central room and plumped for the middle one directly in front of me. The door opened towards me, I paused, listened again and stepped through. I had entered an inner hallway with what were probably bedroom doors at each end. When it comes to heights I always prefer to have the drop to my left, I chose the right hand door. I held my breath and slowly turned the doorknob. I was in complete darkness and stood absolutely still. I heard the deep heavy breathing, smelt urine and could just make out the shape of the wheel chair inside the door. I backed out.

I tiptoed to the other door and entered, not a sound. I closed the door behind me and switched on my pencil torch. The thin beam of light splayed around the room. Cord's domain. The walls were hung with posters of Che Guevara, Arnold Schwarzenegger and, over the bed, Adolph Hitler! The woman needed help; I sincerely hoped that somehow I could find a way to prove she was not related. The dressing table was very orderly, in fact the whole room would have passed inspection by the most discerning sergeant major. I eased open the top drawer of the dresser and found it to be full of newspaper cuttings carefully clipped together and dated. There were maps, a compass, several packets of cigars and, oh glory, her diary! I stuffed it inside my shirt, buttoned it up securely and switched off the torch. I stepped back through the door, turned and carefully closed it behind me. I immediately felt the presence and froze.

"I have a gun pointed at your head!" The deep hoarse whisper filled the hallway with an icy menace. "Turn around very slowly with your hands on your head!"

I obliged trying to ignore the sharp scratch of the diary's metal clasp as it dug into my skin and slid down to my waist inside my shirt. The figure in the wheelchair was hunched and small. The gnarled hand holding the gun was very steady and the black glinting angry eyes stared at me from between twitching eyelids. Its other hand reached for the light switch and the hallway was flooded in blinding light. Unbelievably, the person was dressed in what appeared to be a rather dishevelled nun's habit, which had obviously been slept in.

"Who the hell are you and what are you doing creeping about my home?" The hoarse whisperer asked fiercely, then immediately burst into a fit of chesty coughing. When she had stopped coughing I told her honestly that I was Joanna Wilde and that I was staying at the house. This seemed to have quite an adverse effect on the poor woman and the coughing became quite violent. I sensed the opportunity to make a dash for it but she was too quick for me. "Don't even think about it, I do know how to use this!" she croaked flashing the gun at me. "Go into the living room and pour me a large whisky!"

She followed me through the door in her wheel chair watching my every move. "Pour yourself one, it might help you relax."

"No thanks, I can't stand the stuff, do you have anything else?" I asked rather too rudely. A chesty laugh. "Is there anything else?" Another fit of coughing.

"You ought to see a doctor about that cough, it's no wonder you're in a wheelchair!" I realised that I had made a very stupid statement, but it is amazing what comes out of one's mouth when faced with a gun wielding crippled nun!

"Is Emma here with you?" The question was totally unexpected and threw me completely. "How do know about Emma?" I gasped.

"Cordelia has told me all about you, did you realise you were sisters?" Another question.

"Emma is in England and yes," I sighed, "I have only just found out about Cord, I had no idea. It is less than two months ago that I found out about my father's other life, nothing seems to shock me anymore."

She sat in the semi-darkness and continued to stare at me. "Shall I turn on a lamp? We can barely see each other" I asked and started to rise.

"Not on my account" she whispered "I'm blind as a bat. If you want some light, put on the small lamp beside you." I obliged. The room was now bathed in a gentle low wattage glow. Her corner of the room remained in semi-darkness. "Why did you come to live with Cord?" I prompted.

"I looked after her and now she looks after me. I have taught her everything

I know and now she's very much in charge of things." A low chortle followed by a burst of coughing. "I'll put the gun away now, I don't think we intend to harm each other do we?" Another cough.

We sat in silence for a full minute and I realised with some amusement that I had been held at gunpoint by a blind nun. She seemed to sense my amusement and made it plain that she did not need eyes to be able to hit her target. She asked why I had been in Cord's room and I told her about how Cord had attacked me, I used this reason for wanting to get my own back at her by 'ransacking her room - tearing down posters' that sort of thing. She seemed genuinely concerned and promised to have words with her. I said that it might make things even worse between us if she did. She asked me more about Emma 'Cord's niece' and seemed remarkably interested in her. She said that she and Cord were 'family' and would like me to feel part of that family. The thought of it made me sick to the stomach. We must have been talking for some time before I remembered the diary; I was desperate to get it back to my room. I said I should leave soon as Cord would be seriously unhappy to find me there. On this subject she agreed.

I stood and the gnarled hand reached out of the darkness for mine. "Come and see me again," she whispered and held onto my hand for an uncomfortably long time. I promised I would, opened the sliding door and came face to face with my sister! With almighty force she thumped me in the chest sending me flying backwards into the room. I crashed into the sideboard sending the whisky and glasses splintering across the floor. Violent coughing erupted from the dark corner.

Cord swung round and rushed to the spluttering whisperer. "Father, Father are you all right, what has she done to you?" "Stupid bitch!" the whisper had deepened into old man speak. "Joanna always had the brains. All you ever had was a thick head and an itchy trigger finger!"

Cord slowly turned towards me. "I should have killed you in Malacca but 'Daddy' said no! Oh, I have brains all right, I've been running the business for five years now and very successfully. I warned him about the Prince going to see you in England, knew that you would take the bait." She swung back to face our Father. "We must kill her now Father, you can't let sentimentality get in the way, she'll ruin everything!"

Slowly the wheelchair moved out of the corner and into the light. My dead father reached up with his good hand and removed the headdress. A quarter of a century had passed and it showed. The same dark eyes peered out of a sunken liver spotted face and the once jet black hair was brylcreamed back into grey and yellow thin curls at the nape of his neck. Despite this, he was completely recognisable and it took my breath away.

"Sadly I am genuinely blind and me knees were shot away by Abdullah, twelve years ago. As I'm as old as the hills and by rights should be dead anyway, I can't really complain." He had retained his Devonshire accent, his voice was older, shakier but the same.

"Cordelia, clear up the glass from the floor and get some fresh glasses and whisky from the kitchen. Find Joanna that bottle of gin you were given last Christmas." Cord hissed her disapproval and found a dustpan and brush for the glass. When, at last we were all seated with filled glasses and lighted cigarettes we attempted to communicate in a rational manner. I was twenty two when I had last smoked a cigarette, this seemed like a good time to start again! I inhaled deeply on the untipped weed and promptly retched which Cord took great delight in. The second puff was easier and I followed it with a large gulp of neat gin. Cord slowly began tapping her red talons on the arm of her leather armchair and then reached over to the glass topped coffee table to replenish her already empty glass. My father's face had gradually split where his mouth was and he began leaning forward with a wide hideous smile on his face. All his teeth had been removed in his thirties and replaced with flashing white false ones. He was now displaying a pair of sunken blue gums. I shuddered and took another mouthful of gin.

"Well, ain't this nice?" my father dribbled. "My two girls here together at last, I didn't expect this to happen in my lifetime, I am well pleased."

"Speak for yourself father, I don't want her here, or anywhere come to that!" Cord hissed through clenched teeth.

"Now just you relax my beauty. Joanna could be very helpful to us, I told you she had brains and we need someone we can trust to advise us on our investments!" he wheezed. "Joanna is family, blood is thicker than water, you wouldn't let us down now would you me lovely?"

"Of course not father, as you say we're family" I heard myself say. "What do you want me to do?"

"Bring your chair next to me, I want to feel you close, come and hold your old dad's hand." He lifted his good arm and frantically beckoned me towards him. My chair was on casters, which slid stiffly and squeakily towards him. I sat down and put my hand in his. His fingers were stained a deep orange, from years of heavy smoking and his breath smelt foul. I tried hard not to shudder, it was like holding the hand of the undead, which was not far from the truth. He prompted me to tell him all about myself and Emma, he seemed completely oblivious to Cord who had been pacing the floor and constantly peering out of the French doors. At last he seemed satisfied and put his head back on the headrest of the chair. Cord took advantage of this pause in the conversation and complained that it was getting light. She was afraid that I would be missed if I did not return to the house as soon as possible. The last thing they wanted, she said, was for a search party to be raised.

"Father, I should go. I can't tell you how wonderful it is to find you still alive." I lied. "But Cord is right. I'll come and see you again tonight and we can discuss the investment side of things." I kissed him on the cheek and followed Cord out onto the veranda. I turned and smiled at the hideous shrunken vision in the wheelchair and saw the glisten of tears on his cheeks.

Cord tugged at my sleeve. "Get a move on wimp, I'll walk you as far as the bridge and keep your head down!" she whispered.

We stood up in the shadow of the bridge and she kept a tight hold on my arm. For a full half minute she scanned the area with her piercing eyes and listened intently for any unusual sounds. The river had dropped a little but continued to pound against the wooden struts of the bridge.

"Perfect" she said and turned to face me. "Father is a sentimental old fool. I'm in charge now despite what he says. I know exactly what you are up to pretty sister, this time I make the decision." I saw the madness in her eyes and, too late, heard the spring of the flick knife. I tried to move away but she was too quick for me. Her arm swung back and the blade plunged into my stomach. I felt winded as if by a knuckle duster and doubled up. Everything else became slow motion. I felt the wind and the whistle of a bullet as it whizzed past my left cheek and saw the triumphant glint in her eyes turn to surprise and then shock. The side of her head seemed to explode; blood, skin and hair flying into the mist and then, like a rag doll, she fell sideways into the reeds. I heard the rush of footsteps and strong arms were preventing me from collapsing onto the wet grass. Numerous men in combat gear were leaping over the balcony and through every visible window of the cottage. I could not believe my eyes.

"Joanna, darling, don't try to move." Dominic held me close and then lifted me into his arms. There was a small trickle of blood on my shirt and, although I felt no pain, the realisation that I had been stabbed suddenly hit home. He was carrying me back towards the cottage and, as we neared the steps to the veranda, a dark swarthy man in combat gear came out through the door. "He was alone, Dominic, it's safe to bring her in." Laurent smiled at me and winked. "Take her through to the room on the left." My head was reeling, I just could not take it all in, everything had happened so fast. My Father sat bent forward in his wheelchair, his head in his good hand. He did not look up as Dominic carried me through to Cord's bedroom. He laid me gently down on the bed and raised his finger to silence me.

"Get some warm water in here and some bandages!" He was shouting now. I looked down at the knife still protruding from just below my ribs but saw only a little blood.

"Lie absolutely still Joanna, I'm going to slowly unbutton your shirt." He was back beside the bed and Laurent was at his side with a bowl of water. The bloodied shirt was unbuttoned and then there was a pregnant pause. "Oh, my God!" I cried. "Is it that bad?"

I looked pleadingly at Dominic and then at Laurent, their lips began to tremble and then they started to laugh! I did not dare look at the knife and at last Dominic calmed down and leaned over the wound. He raised his arm and in his fist was the handle of the knife, the blade was embedded in Cord's plump diary! The men grinned uncontrollably and it was infectious. I grinned back and then we were all laughing. I swung my legs off the bed, stood and hugged both men in turn. "How come you're both dressed in combat gear?" I dared to ask.

"It's a long story, darling." Dominic smiled. "All will be revealed, but first we have to deal with your Father."

Chapter 24

"Would you ladies care for some freshly made lemonade?" Mrs Lee's shadow temporarily blocked out the sun, which had for the last twenty minutes been turning English skin into a slightly redder shade of freckled brown. Susie, already a beautiful golden brown, seemed to be just gently deepening her all over glow. Below us the men were about to begin their tennis match. Both dressed in white with black baseball hats they stood at the net about to toss a coin. "Heads, I win, I'll let you serve. My being the better player, I don't want to take an unfair advantage." Dominic tossed two balls to his opponent and swaggered confidently to the baseline. Laurent turned and after bouncing the ball a few times with his racket, prepared to serve.

"Ace!" Shouted an excited Susie.

"I wasn't ready to receive, for god's sake!" Dominic snarled angrily. "He'll have to play a let."

Dominic returned the second serve but with some considerable difficulty. Laurent was already at the net and the ball was smashed hard just inside the baseline. The first set thankfully went with serve and the two gladiators were persuaded to take a break by the attentive Susie. Both men sat on the grass in the shade, at a forty five degree angle to each other, refusing to speak.

"Look at them" laughed Susie "Like a couple of spoilt schoolboys."

I settled back on my lounger and sighed deeply, this was really heaven. Then my mind started to drift back over the events of the last three days, still quite unable to believe that it hadn't all been a dream.

....

After my Father had been arrested and taken to Police Headquarters in KL, Cord's body was removed and taken to the mortuary. She had been declared dead at the scene from a single bullet to the side of the head. I had formerly identified her and then was later asked to sign a statement confirming that the arrested man had indeed been George Worme, international assassin and gun smuggler. Laurent, it turned out, was a senior officer with Interpol put in charge of the final capture and arrest of George Worme. Interpol had been alerted when the Prince had arrived in England and had subsequently put him under surveillance for the whole of time he was in the country. My home had been very discreetly searched whilst I had been out. The photograph of my father had been found and my record of the Princes visit, so carefully typed on my computer, gave Interpol enough reason to believe that my father may still be alive. His body was exhumed and dental records proved, without any shadow of a doubt, that the poor devil in the ground was not my father.

From that moment on I had been followed and every phone call had been monitored. Dominic believed, and I had to agree with him, that the Prince had hoped I would take the bait and want to dig deeper. We were convinced that, in his dying days, he had wanted my father to be found, but could not bring himself to expose him personally. On the evening of the day of my father's arrest, I had been allowed to visit him in his cell. He was surprisingly comfortable in a hospital type bed and was being attended by a male nurse. Looking much older than a man in his mid-seventies, the sunken face on the pillow had a sickly purple and yellow hue to it. The male nurse placed a chair next to the bed and motioned me to sit.

"Miss Wilde, your father has been asking for you. He is very sick and is suffering from advanced emphysema, I'm afraid there is little we can do for him." He placed his hand on my shoulder and quietly left the room.

"Joanna, my lovely, is that you?" The hand of the undead slid, like an uncoiling snake over the bedcover. I put my hand over it and said yes.

"My clever girl, you were the one to find me. Not even Interpol could have done it without you." His face split into a purple gummed grin and he started to snigger, bits of spittle darting out over his blue lips. "Come closer, my petal, there are things I need to say, secrets between just you and me."

I leant forward but recoiled quickly as he burst into another of his chest wrenching coughs. A bottle of water was standing unopened on the bedside table. I unscrewed the cap and filled a glass with it, then lifting my father's head placed it to his lips. "It be whisky I need, whisky. Can you get me some petal, next time you come in?" I said that I would and waited for him to settle. He clenched my hand and continued with his "secrets".

"Them Interpol, will have found all the evidence they need to convict me of running a world-wide organisation. It was all there, at the cottage. I kept all the records, names, places, dates the lot. What they don't know is where I stashed all the money, but bloods thicker than water an' I know I can trust my Joanna. I want you and Cordelia to be friends, she'll take you to where it be hidden. You need to move it into one of them special bank accounts; the Cayman Islands or somewhere."

He relaxed his hand and seemed to shrink deeper into the bed. Sighing deeply he asked to take a short rest before he continued. He slipped into agitated sleep, his eyes flickering open every so often, then he would grab at my hand again looking for reassurance that I was still there. About ten minutes later he roused himself and called my name. "I'm still here father" I assured him.

"You probably hate me, my pretty. Letting you think I was dead. I had no choice you see, I left the Princess safe with the nuns so as I could return to England. I had arranged for the two of us and the sprog, to slip out of Singapore and disappear to South America, but I had to kill off George Worme first." Intrigued, I encouraged him to tell me more.

"When I got back to the nuns place, I found the Princess dead, the love of my life dead, dead! For the first time in my life I prayed to God, got down on my bloody knees and asked him what to do. Then this nun comes in with the sprog, all wrapped up and cosy like. I knew then that was a sign, the sprog should stay with them, be given a decent upbringing. I couldn't take it with me, not without its mother. So I settled a wodge of money on the nuns and sent the Princess back

to where she belonged." His breathing had become very laboured and his next bout of coughing shook the bed. Anxious to hear the rest of the story I sat patiently and waited for him to settle again.

"I spent the next ten years earning a good living," he continued. *"I was in demand until my eyesight started to give me jip. I trained others to use the gun, all types of gun. I sent them all over the world on assignments and then my lungs started to get the better of me. I needed someone I could trust to run things for me, to be my eyes and ears. I went back to Singapore to get Cordelia, can always depend on family, bloods thicker than water, ain't it?"*

"I think Mr Worme should rest now." The nurse had quietly re-entered the room carrying a small plastic cup containing medication. "A senior officer will be coming to question your father in half an hour's time, these tablets will help settle his condition and regain a little strength. You may return again in the morning after ten O'clock."

I kissed the corpse like creature, which was my father, promising to return in the morning. Max and Dominic were waiting for me in reception.

"Dinner for the beautiful lady, I think," smiled Dominic putting his big protective arm around my shoulders. We repaired to an adjacent restaurant taking a corner booth where we could converse discreetly.

"Well, how did it go?" asked an eager Max.

"He's dying of emphysema, I don't believe he's going to be with us for much longer"

"Well, seeing he's been dead for over a quarter of a century it's amazing that he's still breathing!" roared Dominic.

I tried my best not to join Max in laughing at the rather sick joke and continued. "He's got a considerable amount of money stashed away somewhere, he wants me to join forces with Cord and move it into some safe bank deposit somewhere."

"But Cord is dead, you obviously haven't told him yet." Max frowned.

"I want him to finish his story, to fill in all of those gaps. I want him to explain why he was so cruel to my mother and how he came to be living in that cottage. What I don't want is for him to go into a grief stricken state of mind before I know everything there is to know." I took a large mouthful of the red wine that had been poured for me.

"I understand totally." Max smiled and clicked his fingers in the air. "Now how about getting some service over here, I'm starving."

After ordering I turned to Dominic and looked into his deep blue eyes. How I loved this man and what a terrible waste of the last twenty five years. He smiled as if reading my thoughts and took my hand. "I have a lot of questions to be answered as well, you two." I said very firmly, after dragging my eyes away from Dominic's gaze. "How long have you known about Laurent's true identity?"

"The truth is, Joanna, Max only knew half an hour before I did and that was just before the 'house arrest' thing." Dominic shook his head. "I was amazed and pretty angry when Max arrived at the house with Laurent and his deputy in tow. I am afraid Laurent was assigned to get as close to you as possible and only to reveal his identity when it became absolutely necessary. He, Laurent, believed that we were very close to unearthing your father. By allowing those involved to think that you were implicated in Hussein's murder, he hoped it just might bring him to the surface. As it was, your own determination to solve the mystery found him anyway."

"But how come a small army arrived at the cottage just in time?" I asked.

"You were seen climbing down from the balcony and the locket Laurent gave you has a homing device, he was alerted immediately. There was no way that I would be excluded from any rescue team, I just thank god for the diary stuffed inside your shirt!" Dominic's eyes gleamed with emotion.

Who would have thought that Cord's own diary would have prevented her from killing me? I had to smile at the irony of the situation. I supposed that at some point the reality of the near death thing might hit home, but for the moment all I felt was enormous relief. The food arrived and I was amazed at how hungry I was. We drank three bottles of wine between us, the greater part having been sunk by Max and then hailed a taxi to take us back to Dominic's house.

"Sleep with me tonight, Joanna. Susie is staying with friends and its Mrs Lee's night off, not that I care who knows." Dominic and I stood at the top of the stairs, the house was quiet apart from the snoring Jason in his basket outside Dominic's door.

"Then come into my room," I smiled, hiding the fact that sleeping in his marital bed was not something I could happily deal with. After making love, Dominic fell into a deep, apparently untroubled sleep. I lay in his warmth trying to shut out the awful thought of breaking the news to Susie. Dominic had absolutely no doubts at all that Susie would be able to deal with it, but I could not be so sure. I woke to find myself alone with a shaft of bright light waving backwards and forwards across the opposite wall caused by the gently moving curtains. I reached for the bedside clock and was shocked to find that I had slept until nine thirty!

Two places were laid in the breakfast room with a single red rose on one of the napkins. I wandered out into the kitchen and found Mrs Lee singing away to some Asian music on the radio.

"Ah, Miss Joanna." Beamed the adorable Mrs Lee. "Mr Dominic has walked down to the lake with Satan. He said not to wake you but to send you after him when you are up. The sun is already very hot, please to take one of the hats from the boot room."

As when I first stepped off the plane in Singapore, the air outside felt like the blast of a hot jet engine. By the time I found Dominic and Satan my shorts and shirt were soaked in perspiration. Dominic sat under a young chestnut tree idly throwing a stick into the lake for Jason to retrieve. The beautiful dripping four legged friend rushed to greet me, his bottom wiggling and his tail wagging all at the same time. Dominic heaved himself to his feet and opened his arms in welcome.

"Come and sit here, I've got a flask of chilled orange juice ready." I sat cross-legged on the tartan picnic rug and drank thankfully from the flask in the shade of the tree. Dominic threw Jason's stick out over the water and we watched the golden dog leap enthusiastically after it. "This is my favourite spot," Dominic sighed. "It's the nearest thing to the English countryside, don't you think?" I could not disagree with him. "It's beautiful Dominic, really lovely." Suddenly I felt a pang of homesickness. "There's no reason for you to stay away from England any more, you can come and visit me whenever you choose. You will come and meet Emma as soon as possible won't you?"

"Of course, I can't wait. But there's no question of my visiting you, if we're going to be married then we never need to be apart again. Do you want to get married in England or here in KL?" he grinned flashing his pearly white teeth.

I was dumb struck, this was all moving too fast. "Dominic, I never wanted any man the way I wanted you. That's why I never married, could never settle into another relationship. I can't think of anything I want more than to spend the rest of my life with you, but first things first. You have to tell Susie."

"I know" he cupped my face in his hand and kissed me gently on the mouth. "I am a little nervous about breaking the news. When I told her about your coming to stay, I did not mention our previous relationship. Now she is going to discover that I have a child in England, older than herself! Nevertheless, she is a wonderful girl and I know she will recover from the initial shock and move forward. She has her whole life ahead of her and being tied to an old codger like me is not ideal for a young intelligent beautiful woman, which of course she is."

I marvelled at Dominic's common sense approach, but he did still care about her in fact love her, but not enough to want to spend the rest of his life with her.

"Let's go back to the house and have breakfast. Susie should be back just before lunch, we'll break the news to her then." Dominic reached for my hand and Satan led the way back along the shady lakeside walk and then into the heat of the midmorning sun towards the house. I did not have the appetite for breakfast.

Chapter 25

I heard a car arrive and two car doors slam. Susie was not alone, she had obviously brought one of her Uni friends back with her. I looked into the dressing table mirror, picked up the silver hairbrush and tidied my hair. Perhaps I should have left the moment Dominic had suggested telling Susie, I would be ruining her life, where would she go? She did have her mother, Chor Ling, in Singapore. Perhaps it would be best if I returned to England now, giving her time to adjust to the situation and to start a new life. What about university and all her friends here, Dominic must find her somewhere to live in KL.

Then, to my horror, the door burst open and Susie herself rushed into the room. "Joanna, I've brought my friend Laura to meet you. Her mother is English and she was born in London, can she come in?"

"Yes, yes of course," I found myself stammering. The short, slightly tubby blond girl was pulled into the room and plonked down on the end of my bed next to Susie.

"Go on, ask her!" Prompted Susie.

"Ask me what?" I found myself smiling at the nervous girl who was twisting the end of her long blond pony-tail in her fingers.

"Do you know Simon Le Bon, he's the lead singer with Duran Duran?" Her eyes were wide with expectation. I thought of Emma at that moment and having taken her to two live concerts in the eighties, I had to say yes.

"Oh my god, Oh my god!" Laura was bouncing up and down on the end of the bed.

"Can I join the party?" A grinning Dominic stood leaning against the door-post, his right hand in his trouser pocket. Susie rushed over to Dominic and hugged him. "This is Dominic, drool as much as you like, all the girls do although I can't think why!" Laura was obviously impressed.

Laughing, Dominic spanked Susie on the bottom and shooed her out of the room along with the blushing Laura.

"I think we had better postpone the announcement" I sighed "Susie's rather preoccupied."

"On the contrary, I think it will be good for her to have a friend here. I'll organise Laura to help Mrs Lee in the kitchen for ten minutes and I'll take Susie into my study. Five minutes, OK?" He kissed me gently on the cheek and left the room.

The walk down the stairs and along the hall to the study was the longest journey I could remember ever having taken. Susie was sat in one of the leather armchairs, facing the French windows, with her knees wrapped inside her arms under her chin.

"Dominic tells me he has something very important to say, it must be serious if we're having brandies before lunch!" Susie attempted a flickering smile. "He isn't seriously ill is he Joanna, has he told you anything?"

I also attempted to smile as Dominic handed me my glass and then positioned himself on the arm of my chair.

"There is nothing wrong with me sweetheart, but what I do have to tell you may come as rather a shock," Dominic said calmly.

All three of us took a large gulp of brandy. "Has it got something to do with Joanna? I've had this strange feeling ever since she arrived that there was something between you two, one minute you're friends and the next you're at each other's throats!"

"Yes it has everything to do with Joanna, Joanna and I....." But before Dominic could explain further she was on her feet. "I knew it, I just knew it!" She squealed.

Dominic leapt to his feet and grabbed her shoulders. Gently he put her back into her chair and asked her to remain calm. "Please Susie, it is not what you think, Joanna and I have a history going back to when I was a young marine, even before I came to Malaysia."

Susie curled back up into her chair and as Dominic's story unfolded her eyes became wider and her jaw began to drop. "...My decision to stay in Malaya was made after I discovered that Joanna had aborted the baby... you know the rest of the story. Then just two weeks ago I came face to face with Joanna again after twenty five years. Only three days ago, I discovered that her father had lied and that the baby was born a healthy girl. Joanna named her Emma. She is just a few years older than you."

Dominic quickly moved to the arm of Susie's chair and took her hand. She looked first at Dominic and slowly turned to face me. Her eyes were filling with tears and a huge lump rose into my throat. She uncurled her legs, hauled herself to her feet and with glass in hand walked slowly over to the open French windows. Her long golden hair billowed behind her in the hot tropical breeze and when at last she turned back to face us her face was streaming with tears.

Dominic and I stood and waited "Does this mean that the two of you are back together again?" The voice was small and child-like.

"I was about to tell you ..." But Dominic was silenced by an almighty squeal. Susie was laughing and crying at the same time, we both rushed towards her. "Then I have a big sister, oh heaven, I have always wanted a sister!"

Stunned by what I was hearing I stopped in my tracks and stared in disbelief as Susie flung herself into Dominic's arms. "You will marry Joanna won't you, you absolutely must!"

Then she was hugging me and dancing me around the room. Dominic was laughing and shouting for Mrs Lee, whilst my head was reeling with the brandy and the excitement. Susie was Dominic's *daughter*, of course, it suddenly all made sense! I had automatically assumed that he was still married and of course to Susie, I had no reason to think otherwise! I was overwhelmed with happiness, I would not be losing Susie's friendship, and I would be gaining a daughter! Susie had rushed out of the room in search of Laura, "I have a sister, I have a sister!" Her voice echoed back along the hallway from the kitchen. Mrs Lee arrived with champagne and Dominic was on the phone. "Get everyone over here now! I've got an important announcement to make." Then I was in an enormous bear hug, "I told you it would be all right, you will marry me now won't you Joanna?" What could I say? I could never admit to thinking that Susie was his wife now could I? "I think the engagement has been long enough," I laughed. "Of course I'll marry you, you big ape."

As you can imagine, a lot of champagne was drunk over the next few hours, even Laurent had joined in the celebrations having arrived with Max. There was still one more hill to climb, however, I had yet to break the news to Emma. Doing it over the telephone did not seem right, not only did she have a new sister but a rediscovered father as well.

Emma was very different to Susie, I felt that she may feel uncomfortable sharing me with a half-sister. She was very possessive, had been used to being the centre of attention and enjoyed it. I suppose I had spoiled her terribly over the years, she had been my only link to Dominic. I would wait until I returned to England, perhaps take Dominic and Susie with me.

"So, the love of my life is to marry another man." Laurent was standing close behind me and I could feel his breath on my neck. "Will you drink champagne with a broken man, ma Cherie?"

"I'm sorry Laurent, but you can hardly expect me to cheerfully clink glasses with you after the way you used me." I hissed.

"It was not my brief to fall in love with you Joanna that came naturally." He whispered. "But I am not, how you say, a bad loser. I will be returning to London at the end of the week and hope that we can part as close friends." He lifted my hand to his lips and kissed my finger-tips. I felt the thrill go to the pit of my stomach.

"What are you doing hogging the only attractive eligible man in the room, Joanna?" Susie had slipped her arm through Laurent's and with fluttering eyelashes led him out into the garden. I smiled, he would be quite a catch for any woman but I doubted if, in his profession, he would ever commit to just one.

"Joanna," Max had taken hold of my elbow. "I've just had a call from police headquarters; your father has taken a turn for the worse and is asking for you." I had completely forgotten about him!

Dominic drove me into KL and parked at police headquarters. I wanted to visit my father alone, as his meeting Dominic again after all those years, might cause him to clam up with the rest of his story. He had been moved to a small hospital wing but remained under full police guard. After I had left the previous evening, he had been interviewed by Laurent. Having nothing left to lose, he had been happy to admit to all the atrocities he was accused of, in fact had been proud of it. I, on the other hand, did not intend to let him die a happy man.

"Joanna, is that you?" His blind eyes rolled around in his head as if trying to focus on something.

"Yes Father, it's me. How are you?" I said, sounding like a doting daughter.

"Have you spoken to Cordelia? We need to get the money moved." He attempted to lift his head but flopped back with an exasperated sigh.

"I've made all the arrangements for moving the money, father, but Cord is under arrest and won't play ball with me. She is refusing to tell me where the money is hidden."

A heavy burst of coughing ensued until finally he pulled me closer to him and whispered. "Remember, my lovely, bloods thicker than water. Did you bring the whisky?"

I produced a half bottle from my shoulder bag, obtained earlier from Dominic, and unscrewed the cap. Saliva seeped out of the side of the blue slit in the face and a shaking hand clutched at the air for the bottle. He took three gulps before coughing back half of it and promptly washed back the phlegm with a further mouthful. "Ah, you are a good un Joanna, now you listen carefully."

Over the next five minutes he explained where the money was and how I could retrieve it. I promised that I would move it to a safe account in the Cayman

Islands. He wanted me to have some of the money now to buy some "pretty things" for Emma. Then, at last he fell into a fitful sleep, waking every so often to check that I was still there.

Just when I thought I would get nothing else from him, he started to speak in a wheezy whisper. *"I loved your Mother, but she hated me. I married her because you were on the way, but she refused to let me near her after our wedding day. One day she said that she should have married Abdullah, so I hit her. Her nose bled and her eye blackened up. I could only take my comforts by force, I was her husband, and I had rights."* I felt myself start to tremble inside but outwardly kept my cool and let him continue.

"When Abdullah turned up again I forced her to keep quiet, pretend she was happy. He offered me work in Malaysia, maybe it was his way of getting me away from her, and maybe it weren't." A bout of coughing and choking followed, then a nurse came to clean him up and give him an injection. I was asked not to stay too much longer, the injection would soon make him sleepy anyway.

"Joanna, whisky!" I put the bottle back into his grabbing hand and watched him swallow, dribble and spit a large quantity.

"Father, what happened after you returned to Singapore to fetch Cordelia?" I prompted.

"She was gone. Gone to live with Abdullah, can you believe it? I fucked that Mother Superior, smashed up her bloody office and her." The hideous sneer was revolting and the spittle jetted out over the sides of his mouth.

"I had nowhere else to go so I rang Abdullah up. I was angry, he had stolen my daughter and I wanted her back. He said he would come and get me, let bygones be bygones, I could go and live with him too. When we got to his house, Cordelia was a grown woman and she was pleased to see me. Her and me, we moved into the cottage and I taught her to shoot and handle herself. Her friend Yeuw, he learnt too. Then one night the Prince, he called me into his big snooker room and challenged me to a game. He got very drunk and said he had never forgiven

me for what I had done to him, he took a gun an' shot me knees away!"

"Who killed Abdul, Father, was that Yeuw?" I asked. With his being in full flow I thought he would be easily coerced, but his grip suddenly tightened around the bottle and he forced the spout up under my chin. *"I never meant to hurt me family, bloods thicker than water ain't it? I'll tell you, but you best keep it a secret or else."* At that moment I felt at first hand the deep seated evil that was my father, if he had been fit and well I would have taken him very seriously indeed.

"Cordelia wanted to do the job herself. We had spies following you and when you arrived in Malacca we reckoned that Hussein might show himself. Silly bugger thought I was dead!" His attempt to laugh resulted in a rib cracking bout of coughing and then he began to vomit blood. Two nurses rushed to the bed and asked me to leave. However, there was one last thing I wanted to do, then my father could rot in hell for all I cared.

I found Dominic in the canteen drinking tea. "Dominic darling, I want you to come and pay your last respects to my father."

"You have to be joking, the only thing I want to do for your father is punch his lights out!" he snarled.

"Well I think we can do better than that, follow me." Taking Dominic's hand I led him back to my father's room.

The nurses seemed to have settled him down but were not keen to see me back. "There is something important I meant to say to him, it will only take a minute." The nurses agreed to just two minutes and quietly shut the door behind them. I approached the bed and leant over the gasping undead. "Father, I'm still here can you hear me?" He squeezed my hand. "I've brought someone to see you. You remember Dominic don't you, Emma's father, well he's standing beside me right now."

The black squinting eyes flicked open and started rolling around in his head, he could hear me all right. "You lied to Dominic, you told him that I had aborted Emma; for twenty five years I believed he had deserted me. Well I would like you to know that we are about to be married and you're not invited, you're probably going to croak any minute anyway. Oh yes, the other thing I want to say is that Cord is dead, shot whilst trying to stab me to death, what do you think of that then?" I felt my voice rising as Dominic placed his arm around my shoulder and his hand grip my upper arm.

"I've sorted your money out all right, you bastard, it's being handed over to Interpol and we're going to ensure that Hussein's wife will benefit too." Now I was raging. "You killed my Mother just as sure as you had wielded the knife yourself, I hope you rot in hell!" My heart was pounding and the emotion had brought me near to tears.

"That goes for me too, you heap of slime!" Dominic blasted into the face of the dribbling heap.

The heart monitor was sending out loud long bleeps as the nurses rushed into the room, as we walked down the corridor the long steady single bleep of the machine faded into the distance. At last I felt at peace.

Chapter 26

"OK, Tie Break! My serve." Dominic was preparing to serve and Laurent was crouching on the baseline in readiness.

"Ace, brilliant serve!" Shouted Susie.

The tie break went with serve, then at last Laurent lost his service on the eleventh point, and with two almighty crashing aces Dominic took the set.

"Come on you two, it's far too hot for any more tennis!" I called.

"Ah, mais non, Joanna," Laurent shouted back. "We agreed the best of three!"

"It's OK, darling" Dominic grinned, whilst swatting the air with the back of his hand. "We'll only be playing one more set. I'm used to the heat and I should at least give the man a second chance!" And so the gladiators continued.

Susie and I pulled our loungers further back into the shade and we drank some more lemonade.

"I think I'm a little in love with Laurent" Susie sighed.

"I'm not the slightest bit surprised" I smiled. "Be careful though, I understand that he has quite a reputation with the ladies."

I closed my eyes and drifted back into my recent memories recalling that walk down the corridor away from my dying Father. By the time Dominic and I had returned home a call had come from the hospital to confirm that he was dead. We went to the study and sat for a while in silence.

"I assume you have everything on tape so far," Dominic stated rather than asked. "By that I don't necessarily mean a recording of your discussions with your father, but a record for your research file."

"I feel as if I have been living the research, ever since I left England. Oh yes, it's all on record - in my head that is. I will put it all on tape, but quite frankly every single detail is indelibly printed on my brain."

"It's been an amazing experience, darling. You certainly came back into my life with an enormous bang!" Dominic laughed. Then raising his eyebrows, he said, "In more ways than one!"

"You haven't changed a bit Dominic, not a bit!" And we both laughed long and hard.

"Going to let me in on the joke?" Susie arrived carrying a pot of Earl Grey and three cups. "You don't mind if I join you do you?"

"Of course not Susie" I smiled. "Pull up a chair and tell us what you've been up to today."

"Actually, I went out for a late lunch with Laurent after you left for the hospital." Her eyes had glazed over a little and I immediately recognised the signs. "He has a fashion design business in London you know and he's invited me to visit him when we go to England. We are going to England aren't we? I just can't wait to meet Emma."

The father that was Dominic entered the conversation. "I can't say that I'm happy about your friendship with Laurent, I still don't trust the man." He had become physically larger in his chair, his shoulders were raised and his knuckles had whitened where he was gripping the arms of his chair. "You would do better to stick to friends of your own age."

"Oh, honestly Dominic" she laughed, "don't be such an old stuffed shirt, the next thing is you'll be insisting that I call you daddy again!"

"Well, I never approved of your idea for using Christian names in the first place" he said in a rather sulky voice. "What do you think Joanna, what does Emma call you?"

"Mum actually, but that's her choice, I quite like the use of Christian names." I smiled, not daring to let on that the use of the word daddy would have saved me an awful lot of anguish.

"There you are DADDY" she laughed. "You don't stand a chance with Joanna on my side. Here have a cup of tea."

"I'm taking Joanna out to dinner tonight." Dominic announced after a brief sulky silence. "When we get back she'll be sharing my room, I thought it best that you know about the new arrangement."

"I would have been amazed it were not the case, I'm not a child you know!" She looked a little hurt. "So when are you getting married?"

At this point I felt I should have some say on the matter of marriage. "I don't want to rush into marriage, we've only just re-established our relationship, I have yet to break the news to Emma and I would like her to meet you both before any arrangements are made."

"Joanna is right Susie," Dominic said firmly. "We should not be putting her under pressure when there are an awful lot of other things yet to be sorted. The most important thing is that she has said yes. We have funerals to attend not only for Worme and Cord but also for Abdul. Tomorrow morning I suggest that Joanna and I sort out the personal effects at the cottage. I have arranged for Abdul's wife Margaret and the Commander to join us here for lunch and we also need to finalise things with Interpol."

"Yes, I'm sorry." Susie half smiled. "The news was so exciting about Emma and Joanna this morning that my feet have hardly touched the ground!"

When Dominic and I let ourselves into the cottage following morning, it still wreaked of stale tobacco and whisky. Interpol had done a thorough job of removing all the evidence they could find and had left things reasonably tidy. I decided to start with my father's room. The first thing I did was to open the windows to let in some air; despite the humidity it released some of the feeling of claustrophobia and stale tobacco fumes. It was most uncanny to find that he had few personal effects, just like the time of his "first" death. He was still rolling his own cigarettes, had accumulated a few more pairs of socks and underwear and had obviously taken his disguise as a nun very seriously. A spare habit was hanging in the wardrobe and two pairs of size eight lace up boots were under the bed. The most interesting find was an envelope containing well-thumbed photographs of myself and my mother. Also a photograph of the new born Emma cradled in my arms in the maternity ward and finally a picture of my father and the Princess, on a windy beach, smiling happily with their arms around each other. Dominic, meanwhile, had been browsing through the books and videos in the sitting room. He confirmed my father's and sister's complete lack of taste. Mostly paperbacks, westerns, horror and a fair 'sprinkling' of porn.

Cord's personal effects revealed no surprises apart from one. In her jewellery box I found a charm bracelet, which was virtually identical to my own! Something in my recent past had indicated that another similar bracelet existed - of course, Chor Ling had mentioned that she had seen one just like mine, worn by a little white girl. Had Chor Ling visited the orphanage at some point? That had to be the answer.

Back in my room at Dominic's house, I put Cord's charm bracelet on the dressing table. I took mine off and laid them side by side. They were almost identical, one each for his two daughters. Mine appeared rather more worn, I imagined that Cord would have considered her bracelet to be too prissy for her taste and had kept it in her jewellery box. I turned the elephants until they were all facing outwards and realised that the ornate letters on Cord's bracelet were different to my own. Curious, I opened the dressing table drawer and found a notepad and pen. I knew the letters on my bracelet by heart and wrote, J..umbo, M..imi, O..scar, A..dam, G..eorge and M..onique. Cord's bracelet had an extra elephant, seven in total and the letters were, U,B,S,R,E,E and S. This was fascinating, could there be some Far Eastern significance or simply the random carving of the jeweller who had made them? I tried putting all the letters together in rows and then in a circle. I could not make out any particular word, well not in English anyway. Frustrated, I had to conclude that I was probably suffering from an over active imagination. I put the bracelets and my notes in the drawer, showered, changed into a black cotton dress and prepared to greet Abdul's wife Margaret and the Commander. I felt able to face her now, having effected a certain amount of just revenge on my Father. This, however, would not bring her devoted husband back and I prayed that she could find it in her heart not to hate me. I practised a relaxed smile in the mirror and headed for the stairs.

I could hear voices in the hallway and hastened to greet the guests. The Commander was unexpectedly small and indeed no taller than his companion. He was very upright, in crumpled cream lightweight suit and carefully tied paisley cravat. His brown brogues were highly polished and he was supported by a brass handled walking stick. The moment I reached the bottom of the stairs his clean shaven, rosy cheeked face broke into the most charming smile and stepping forward he reached for my hand shaking it warmly. "May I call you Joanna, I really would prefer to dispense with any formalities strait away and I know Margaret feels the same." "Oh yes, please do" I replied, disguising my relief with a wide smile.

"This is Margaret, her English is limited, but she will understand most things you say to her." The Commander reached for her hand and brought her to his side. Margaret bowed deeply and reached out both hands into which I placed both of mine. She was really lovely, the years had etched deep lines into what would have been a very pretty face. Her long white hair had been carefully wound up into a neat bun, which was contained within a black net, and she was dressed in traditional Moslem mourning dress.

"It is a pleasure to meet you Margaret" I smiled. "But I am so sorry that we are meeting in such sad circumstances."

"Please, do come through to the sitting room." Dominic held out his arm and led Margaret gently through to the sunlit room. The Commander and I linked arms and followed in their wake.

"Would you like some refreshment Margaret, a soft drink, tea or perhaps something stronger?" Dominic had shown Margaret to a comfortable sofa and was being the perfect gentleman. "Mrs Lee makes a delicious lemonade, perhaps you would like to try it."

Margaret nodded with a little flickering smile and we all agreed to participate. The Commander sat beside her and I made myself comfortable in one of the large armchairs. Dominic, having ordered the lemonade pulled up a leather swivel chair to join us.

"Before we begin, Margaret has asked me to say that on no account does she blame either of you for Abdul's death." The Commander began. "She wants you to know that Abdul had told her of his plans and that he knew the risk he was taking in going to see you. She says that at last he will be at rest knowing that justice has been done."

"Thank you, Margaret." I said, nodding with genuine gratitude. "You have helped to ease my troubled mind. Are you aware that my father is now definitely dead, as is Abdul's murderer, his daughter Cordelia?"

"Yes, yes." Margaret's small high pitched voice was heard for the first time. "Him, Mr Max, he bring us news." I could see tears welling up in her eyes. I asked how soon she expected to be able to return Abdul to Malacca. Apparently, it was to be at least another twenty four hours before this could be confirmed. Her eldest daughter would be making the arrangements.

Mrs Lee arrived with the lemonade and we took our filled glasses out onto the veranda. Margaret visibly relaxed as she pointed to various parts of the garden and was delighted to find that lunch was to be served al fresco under a shady awning. By the time she left, she and I had formed an unbreakable bond, we had after all both been unwilling victims of the same evil man. Dominic and I accepted her request to join her in Malacca for the funeral.

After we had waved our goodbyes, I took Dominic to my room. I could not get the bracelets out of my mind and wanted to show him. I laid them out side by side on the dressing table again and placed my notes with them. Dominic pulled up a chair and cupping his chin in his left hand, doodled around for a bit on a fresh piece of paper. "I can't see any Chinese or Malayan word in this, perhaps it's more than one word." "One word that stands out to me is Jumbo." I said, casually. "Emma had a pink soft toy called Jumbo, I think she still has it!"

"OK, that then leaves A-G-M-S-R-E-E-S." Dominic wrote the remaining letters in a line, then in a circle. "AGREE shouts out at you, doesn't it, but then that leaves M-S-S. We could assume that the S's pluralise both words, or perhaps one word. JUMBOS AGREE MS. No, I think we're off track."

"The letters are probably not meant to be anything." I prompted. "You would think though that the bracelets would at least have had the same number of elephants."

"Hang on a minute, let's try for three words. What else can you see in the remaining words, three or four letter words." Dominic was not going to be beaten, I had already witnessed his determination to complete both the Telegraph and Financial Times crosswords every day. He just loved anagrams.

AGE, SEEM, RAG, GASS, GEM, MARE, RAGE, ARSE, GEAR, ARE. He was writing furiously. "Try putting S's on the end of those." I prompted.

At last two of the words stood out, GEMS and ARE. These two words used all the remaining letters apart from one S. "Well, GEMS ARE JUMBOS or rather JUMBOS ARE GEMS, either way both the S's have been used up by making JUMBO plural." Dominic was pleased. "But it's a rather silly sentence."

We sat in silence for a few seconds and then it hit us, we each grabbed a bracelet. "Are you thinking what I'm thinking?" Dominic was grinning broadly.

"I think so. The elephants are Jumbos, the Jumbos are gems - could these fat round elephants hold a secret?" I almost shouted, feeling incredibly excited.

"Let's go down to the study, I've got a magnifying glass there."

I needed no encouragement and we raced down the stairs like a couple of excited schoolchildren. Dominic opened his desk drawer and found the magnifying glass. Switching on the desk lamp he held one of the elephants between his forefinger and thumb and peered at it through the glass.

"YES! Look at this Joanna, you can clearly see a fine welded join where two halves have been sealed together." He handed me the glass and bracelet. Sure enough, what I had believed to be solid figures were in fact hollow, so what was it that made them feel so heavy.

"Right, to the workshop." I followed Dominic's lengthy stride at a jogging pace due to our height difference, around to the back of the garage block and into a spacious high tech armourer's workshop. Vic was whistling happily and filing away at some metal object. He looked up in surprise.

Dominic handed Cord's bracelet to Vic. "Here you are, mate, this should prove to be very interesting. I want you to open up these little blighters so we can see what's inside."

Using a precision laser tool and the aid of magnified eye piece, Vic set to work. It did not take long and I held my breath as he carefully eased the first jumbo apart. I saw the sparkle and then heard Vic gasp. "Christ almighty, there's a diamond in here as big as a marble, fetch me that soft cloth!"

I placed the cloth on the bench and Vic tipped the dazzling gem out. We all stood in stunned silence for at least a full minute until Dominic reached for the bracelets. "Open the rest Vic, let's open the bloody lot!"

Ten minutes later we were drooling over six huge diamonds and seven rubies. The mystery over the ruby and diamond necklace was solved. The dismantled bracelets were solid gold, created, no doubt from the melted necklace. For a quarter of a century two sisters had innocently been joint guardians of one of the world's most valuable pieces of jewellery!

Chapter 27

The gladiators were rubbing themselves down with towels and gulping bottled water. They had just completed a second tie-brake and Laurent had taken the set at 17/15. Dominic was putting the blame on the man who had recently re-strung his two best rackets and had unloaded six more from his enormous kit bag. He proceeded to tap the strings with the side of another racket until at last he seemed satisfied with the one in his right hand. He then insisted on a few practice serves before continuing. Laurent, meanwhile, seemed satisfied with his original racket and sat down on the grass next to Susie.

"Your father, he does not like to lose." He smiled, flashing his sparkling white teeth.

"He hasn't lost yet!" laughed Susie. "In fact I can't remember the last time he was beaten in a three setter!"

"Well, my pretty one, this may well be the time." He kissed her hand, winked at me, strode back down the grass slope and through the wired gate onto the court.

Dominic held up the new ball and proceeded to serve. Laurent just managed to return it, but it was long. The server returned to the base line, adjusted a couple of strings and let forth a blistering ace. He had truly found his form and took the game to love. Laurent struggled to keep his first service game and his legs were beginning to look decidedly heavy. The heat was beginning to take its toll and he inevitably lost his service in the fourth game. At Dominic's instigation, they took a two minute break to 'give the poor guy a breather' and ate a banana each. Then after another towel down and a quantity of water they returned to the court.

Laurent seemed to have renewed his strength and concentration because, to Dominic's horror, he broke serve! Mrs Lee had arrived to clear the glasses and witnessed the last set. She a Susie made a quaint couple jumping up and down squealing at the top of the ha-ha. With a chuckle I rested back onto the lounger and closed my eyes.

....

Following the discovery of the gems, Dominic and I had returned to his study. Quite naturally, we downed a couple of stiff brandies and sunk into the leather armchairs. The glittering gems lay sparkling on Vic's soft rag on the small lacquered table. We both sat leaning forward with our elbows on our knees. If ever silence were to say a thousand words it did so then. Gradually our smiles erupted into grins and then laughter.

"That devious bastard." Dominic roared. "According to Abdul's diary, there were an awful lot of jewellery thefts and you can be certain that your Father will have pocketed a fair share of these."

"His deviousness will have been a direct result of his successful black market days." I shook my head. "I wonder how much Hussein knows about his and my father's cache? Has he accessed the Princes safe yet? He did tell me that he looked after his father's financial affairs and investments, but to what degree that's the question? I got the feeling that he had, at least in recent years, been running the Prince's affairs in a legitimate way. But in saying that I would quite like to have a quiet word with him."

"Yes, I agree, there are so many questions still to be answered." Dominic was nodding. "Why don't you call him, give him your condolences and say that we would like to pop over. In the meantime these little beauties will be better off in the safe."

Hussein sounded pleased to hear from me and suggested we join him for dinner. Dominic looked a little disappointed, but agreed to postpone our planned intimate dinner after a little gentle female persuasion. He insisted on dressing smart but casual, no he was not going to wear a tie, but did slip one into his pocket.

The table had been laid for three in a smaller anti-room off the main dining room. The atmosphere was rather more relaxed than my last visit to the house and we were greeted with warm handshakes.

"Would you care for an aperitif before we dine?" Hussein's butler stood to attention with a tray of filled bubbling champagne glasses and a bowl of stuffed olives. With glasses in hand we were led by the elegant, if rather plump Prince out to a balustraded balcony.

"Do we have something to celebrate or do you always drink champagne before dinner?" I smiled, raising my glass.

"I think we do have something to celebrate and in particular our exciting futures." The Prince raised his glass and we all drank to that. He rested his free hand on the stone balustrade and gazed out over the rose garden towards the cottage in the distance.

"For nearly fifteen years George Worme was living at the bottom of the garden and I had no idea. I was told that Cordelia's Mother Superior had retired and had been invited to live with her." He turned to face us. "I really did not know my father at all. He encouraged me in certain insurgent activities during my immature years and approved much of my work as a writer, but we were never really close. When I entered my thirties I wanted to have a positive role in the running of the estates. I went to college, obtained a degree in business studies and was gradually allowed to take a more senior role within the estate manager's office. In recent years he gave me Power of Attorney to handle his properties and Stock Market investments; I believe that I have done a reasonably good job. You might like to have a look at these Joanna, your experienced view would be appreciated."

"I'm surprised that you know about my fund management background." I felt a little uncomfortable for the first time.

"Oh, yes" He smiled. "When my father finally tracked you down he seemed very pleased to find that you had become a successful lady. Hoare Wilde Fund Managers have an enviable track record in the city of London."

"Your Father was in love with my Mother you know, he actually asked her to marry him. I think I reminded him of her, perhaps he felt proud of me on her behalf." I slipped my hand into Dominic's and gently squeezed it.

"I've asked Joanna to marry me and she has said yes." Dominic smiled into my eyes and squeezed my hand a little tighter. "I'm also very proud of her."

"You are a very lucky man sir, I raise my glass to you both." I felt the embarrassed flush in my cheeks and took a mouthful of the golden liquid.

"Come, let us repair to dinner and we can talk further over some good vintage wine." I took Hussein's arm and was led, with Dominic in our wake to the anti-room.

The round table was beautifully laid with the best crystal and silver. The delicate scent of roses wafted across from the centre display and the small rose watered finger bowls at each setting.

"In Joanna's honour, I have ordered five vegetarian courses all delicately prepared under my personal supervision. We start with marinated goat's cheese in a tossed green salad."

Each course was mouth-wateringly different and in total, we spent nearly three hours enjoying the culinary delights. Vintage wines had been bought up from the Prince's "extensive" cellar, a different one with each course. To further add to the evening Dominic and I learnt a great deal more about Prince Abdullah, than we could ever have hoped for.

"Before he died my father told me a lot of things including his love for Monique." Hussein began. *"He made it quite clear that I was to ensure your safety should you follow him here. Of course, I had no idea that your father was still alive or about his relationship to Cord. My Father did not offer that information. I knew Cord was my half-sister and she always had a way of twisting me around her little finger, at thirteen she was a big eyed skinny girl with long dark hair nothing like the woman she turned out to be. When she was twenty one she took over the running of the domestic side of the estate, this was not too popular with the staff, but my father wanted her to be occupied. She and Yeuw*

have always been inseparable and I had expected them to marry one day; what will become of Yeuw now I wonder? He was obviously a co-conspirator in the murder of Abdul and is still under arrest at central police headquarters."

"Were you aware of the Prince's past relationship with Worme?" Dominic asked as he reached for his glass of Recoulte.

"I was born in 1955 and the friendship was already well established. Worme was even at my parents wedding! I grew up always having him around, he used to play with me, cowboys and Indians, that sort of thing. The last time I saw him was shortly after my mother left; I feel so stupid not having made the connection between them." He took a large mouthful of wine. *"I only really new the truth after my father died. I went to his study the following morning to see if he had left any special instructions other than the legal ones. Locked in his safe was a record of the assassinations and an incredible amount of priceless jewellery, I'm arranging to have these identified and valued at the moment. I assume this does not surprise you."*

I smiled to myself remembering my visit to the study. "I'm afraid it doesn't, Hussein, we have a similar record which was kept by poor Abdul. I do have a confession to make though; I'm afraid I took something from the study, a leather suitcase which was full of letters, very interesting ones."

"So that's where it went!" Hussein raised his eyebrows and smiled. "I had already read them Joanna, it was one of the first things I opened. I think you should keep the ones from Monique but I would like the others returned."

"Thank you Hussein, I appreciate that," I said with genuine gratitude.

"We have to now consider the funeral for both Cord and your Father. She was our half-sister but baptised into the Christian faith. It would seem appropriate to arrange a joint Christian burial don't you think?" Hussein prompted.

"Sod that" growled Dominic "It would be an insult to the church, send them for a burn up and be done with it!" I kicked his ankle.

"I understand your feelings Dominic, the shorter and simpler the ceremony the better. I would welcome your ideas for my mother's belongings, Joanna." Hussein had tactfully changed the subject.

"Her wardrobe is absolutely stunning. I am aware that Zandra Rhodes is in the early stages of planning a museum of fashion in London. I'm sure that the Princess's gowns will be of considerable interest. Other than that I think it may be a good idea to auction her clothes and jewellery in aid of a suitable charity." Deep down I felt that the sooner the Princess's creepy suite was cleared and updated the better.

"Thank you Joanna, is there any chance you could contact this Zandra?" He asked.

I said that I did have her business card and would see what I could do when I returned to England. I also suggested that a professional photographer be drafted in to photograph and log all the outfits. At this point I could tell that Dominic was tiring of the conversation and having had our fill of good food and wine, asked Hussein if perhaps we could take our coffee out onto the balcony.

A great big orange sun was slowly sinking like a broken egg yolk into the distant tree line and, as we settled into the white wicker chairs, I felt an air of sadness about us.

"What do you plan to do with the cottage?" I asked.

Hussein sighed deeply. "It was always the gardener's cottage until Cord went to live there, I see no reason why it shouldn't be again. As regards the rest of this estate, I'm not sure that I want to stay here. There is a house in Mayfair, London that is currently let, and properties in Singapore, New York, Monaco and Ireland. Perhaps I should find myself a wife and start a family, I think the time is now right. Perhaps I should come to England and find a Monique of my own!"

He was obviously already being affected by loneliness having lost both his father and sister in such a short space of time. But his face had now brightened considerably. "You must introduce me to a young Deborah." "I think you mean Debutante!" I laughed. "Yes, yes a deboratant!" he gushed. And we all roared with laughter.

Chapter 28

"It's still going with serve and its 9-8!" Sighed Susie as she flopped back onto her lounger. "Have you been sleeping?" "No, no." I smiled. "Just deep in thought with my eyes closed. I suppose I should pay attention and see the end of the match."

Putting on the floppy straw hat I had borrowed from the boot room earlier, I went and sat on the grass at the top of the ha-ha. The gladiators were soaked in sweat and it was now proving necessary to use their towels after every point. Both men were exhausted but neither would give way. Then it happened, a deep volley from Dominic sent Laurent leaping through the air only to land badly on his racket arm. Five minutes later he had conceded the match and Dominic marched triumphantly up the grassy slope.

"Well done, darling." I gushed. "I will hug you, but would appreciate your having a shower first." Beaming, Dominic swaggered into his personal club house and I turned to look for the defeated Frenchman. Susie had rushed to assist Laurent with his bag and was clucking around him as he dragged himself, chin on his chest, towards me.

"It was the fall, ma petite." I could hear him saying and then looking up at me he spread his hands out and attempted a smile. "I lose again Joanna, I lose again!" "But you lost like a champion, Laurent, you played really well and were a very close second!" I lifted my eyebrows, gave him a knowing smile then the three of us walked together into the comparatively dark interior of the wooden building.

You could have lifted the 'club house' straight out of a private English tennis club setting. The all timber building housed men's and ladies showers, bar and lounge. Four low round tables were each surrounded by canvas directors chairs obviously designed for visiting teams.

Laurent now disappeared to the shower room and Susie had her head in the fridge behind the bar. "What do you fancy Joanna, beer, wine, lemonade...?"

"A beer would go down very well, thanks." I smiled and my thoughts went back to my sacred garden and Dippy after a hard days digging in the vegetable patch. My home seemed like an eternity away.

....

When I had awoken in Dominic's warmth and his big comfortable bed earlier that day, I had lain for quite a while listening to his gentle steady breathing. We had arrived back after dinner the previous evening, to find Susie and Laurent huddled together on the swing seat by the croquet lawn. They had also been out to dinner and then attempted to play a rather tiddly came of croquet. Dominic, the father, had insisted that the mallets, balls and hoops be put away and that Laurent head back to his hotel. I smiled as I remembered Susie jumping to her feet hands on hips, telling Dominic in no uncertain terms that Laurent was staying the night and that the clearing up could be done in the morning. Dominic had risen to his maximum height and turned on Laurent with his raised fist firmly clenched. I had stepped between them and suggested that perhaps Laurent could stay in the guest cottage with Vic for the night.

....

Now, sat in this essentially English setting we waited for the victor and fallen hero to appear. "When are you returning to England Joanna?" Susie's question bounced me back into the real world. "I hope to fly home as soon as the funerals are over, Susie, I must say that I do miss the farmhouse and Dippy. Mind you, I shall miss being here once I'm there, I think there's going to be an awful lot of travelling going on in the future!" "But when you and Dominic are married, won't you come and live here?" Susie was pouting. "It's not that simple Susie. One thing I do know for certain is that I must write a book in Devon. That is where it all began and that is where I must finish it." I smiled at the lovely glum face. "I was going to suggest that the two of you fly back with me and stay for a couple of weeks, what do you think?"

Susie let out one of her long squeals. "Oh yes, yes!" and she was racing over to Dominic and Laurent who, freshly laundered, were heading for the chilled cabinet.

"Joanna wants us to go to England with her, please say we can Dominic." She gushed and placing her arm around Laurent's waist she suggested that all four of us could fly there together.

"It was just an idea Dominic." I prompted. "Perhaps you could stay for a couple of weeks, spend some time with Emma?" His face broke into his wide melting smile and ruffling Susie's hair said that he could hardly refuse.

The sky had darkened quite suddenly and the first drops of rain could be heard on the slate tiled roof, then through the open door came a puffing Mrs Lee and an excited Satan. "This telegram has arrived for Miss Joanna and the courier is waiting for a reply!" She shook the few drops of rain from her brolly and as if on cue, Satan gave himself a good shake as well. Surprised, I stood and took the sealed brown envelope from Mrs Lee and walked over to the open window. The company had, understandably gone very quiet and waited in anticipation for me to reveal the contents of this surprise communiqué. There were just two typed lines and it read:

"Dearest Mum,

At 4.30 pm today, Harry and I were married. Dippy and Finny were witnesses. With much love, Emma. XXX"

I read the message several times and felt the lump rise into my throat. Although I expected them to marry in the near future I was still taken completely by surprise. Then I smiled and remembered the expectant group of people behind me. I turned and my pleased expression brought instant waves of relief to their faces. "Well, what is it?" cried a frustrated Susie and when I told them there was understandably a mix of emotional reactions.

My own confused feelings, however, very quickly turned to delight. Emma and Harry had done what was right for them. I understood their need for a private wedding and was inclined towards doing something similar myself. But what I now needed to do was to get to a phone, and give the newly married couple a call.

"Hi, Mum, you got the message then!" Harry laughed heartily from the other side of the world. "Who gave you permission to call me Mum, stick to Joanna you cheeky sod!" And I returned the laughter.

"Mum, Mum...no go away Harry, I want to speak to Mum!" I imagined the Son-in-law trying to hang on to the phone. "I think I've made a terrible mistake Mum, he's become really bossy over the last 24 hours. You don't mind do you? You do understand don't you? We just couldn't bear the idea of having to invite all those awful relatives and after we had discovered that Bickleigh Castle did weddings, we decided to go for it. Oh it was so lovely, we got married in the armoury and, you remember our friends Bella and Doug, they came as best man and matron of honour...not that way round of course ... Dippy and Finny wore special buttonholes in their collars. I'll have all the photos ready when you come home. When are you coming home?" Then, as so often happened with Emma during telephone conversations I heard the phone crash to the table and she was now shouting at Finny. "Can you believe it, Mum, Dippy has just come dashing through with an old rotted chew and Finny is trying to take it off him!" I sat down on the hall chair and waited.

"Hello Mum, are you still there?" Emma must have realised at last that I had not said a word so far. "Yes, darling, I'm just waiting to get a chance to speak." I answered.

"You're upset aren't you, Oh god I knew you would be, I said this to Harry but he said I was being paranoid." She whined. "Emma, please, if you give me a chance I will tell you exactly how I feel!" I almost shouted.

"You're angry, yes you're angry, but you must see things from our point of view Mum, I really wanted you there but that then meant Harry's mother too and......"
"Emma will you shut up a minute!" Now I was angry. "You always make

assumptions, I sometimes wonder if you really know me at all. Actually I'm delighted, do you hear me Emma, I said I'm delighted!"

For once there was a strange silence at the end of the line then after a few seconds a small voice said, "Are you really, you're not just saying that are you?"

"Please darling." I sighed. "Believe me I am really really delighted, now I would like to speak to my son-in-law again."

"Thank you, Mum, I do love you." Still a small voice.

"I know you do, darling, I love you too." And she was gone.

"Hi, Mum Oops sorry, Joanna I mean. I told her that you would be pleased for us but you know what she's like, over the top with most things. But we love her anyway don't we!" Harry chuckled. "How are things with you?"

"Great thanks Harry, I have to say that I will also have some very exciting things to tell you both when I come home and I'll be bringing two very important people with me." I smiled up at the handsome blond man who was now leaning against the door post with his arms folded across his chest. He smiled back.

As you can imagine, out came the champagne again! We toasted the happy couple and new found friendship. Dominic now accepted Laurent and was willing to give the man the respect he deserved for putting up a tough fight on the tennis court. How boyish, but then how cute!

That evening Dominic and I set about planning the last few days before flying to England. We received news that Abdul's body was being released in the morning and that the funeral would be on Friday morning in Malacca. We proposed, therefore to arrange flights out of Singapore for the following Monday, after spending a couple of nights with Micky and Julie in Singapore. Interpol were happy with the information they had collected and my father's and sister's bodies could also be released tomorrow, Wednesday, for cremation.

Unfortunately, there had been a press release by the police regarding my father's capture and death that afternoon, which meant that the expected short private cremation may be rather more of a public affair than first expected. This then meant that I would have to speak to Emma again to avoid her hearing about George Worme through the media. The sooner we were in England the better. I felt it best to explain the discovery of my father and his subsequent death to Harry, rather than directly to Emma, and this I did early that evening. The news about Dominic and Susie, however, I preferred to keep to myself until I returned to England.

Chapter 29

It was another hot humid day that Wednesday; hard to imagine that it was to be a day for two cremations and the end of an incredible two weeks. My life had changed irreversibly, some things I would have preferred not to have happened but great happiness and the fulfilment of a lost dream had more than compensated.

My man and I walked Satan down to the lake after breakfast. Once in the shade of the young chestnut tree we relaxed on a tartan rug, taking in turns to throw the stick back into the water for the ever enthusiastic golden dog. I talked to Dominic about the farmhouse and my plans for extending the landscaping into the adjacent fields and woodland. He said that he already felt as if he belonged there and wanted to share every bit of my pleasure in the timelessness of the place. We had already realised that neither one of us could be torn away from the homes we had grown to love and that inevitably we would be spending a great deal of time going backwards and forwards. But this held a certain excitement for me, having an extended family in Malaysia gave me an even greater sense of belonging in this great big world. We had also become accustomed to our own space and, as much as I found the thought of ever being separated from Dominic again quite unbearable, I knew that when we were apart it would only be for very short periods.

Dominic lay supported on his elbows gazing out across the water. "The duck population is increasing every year you know, it's very satisfying." He said proudly. "Does the farmhouse have a lake or pond?"
"I would best describe it as a large pond rather choked with reeds." I said, remembering that I still hadn't done anything about clearing it. "It has at least two brown trout, hopefully more by the time I get home."
"I'll clear the pond for you, as you can see you have an expert in the family now!"

He was serious, of course, in fact Dominic had this frustrating way of being good at almost everything, but it was also one of his many attractions.

At 10 O'clock we reluctantly made our way back to the house to change for the funeral service. I had asked, in fact insisted, that I be able to view the bodies before the coffins were closed. I quite naturally, after my past experience, wanted to make absolutely certain that the bodies in the coffins definitely were my father and half-sister!

I held Dominic's hand very tightly as we entered the mortuary. The cold hit us like a sudden sharp frost, emphasising the presence of death. The attendant led us through to a brightly lit anti-room where the simple pine coffins lay side by side on trolleys. The four Chinese pallbearers stood to attention with their hats in their hands and bowed their heads in respect.

I was surprised at the trouble the undertakers had gone to. Despite our request for absolutely no fuss, my deceased father and sister both lay peacefully, as if asleep, in white gowns with their hands crossed in silk lined caskets. A small spray of white rosebuds were entwined in each of their fingers. I nodded to the attendant and watched as the lids were put in place and firmly screwed down. Although this may seem a little neurotic, I then insisted on following the pallbearers and their loaded trolleys through to the small chapel of rest before taking my seat in the front row. I had no intention of taking my eyes off those coffins until they had finally entered the white hot ovens and come out as ashes!

I felt a gentle hand on my shoulder and looked up into the plump smiling face of Prince Hussein. Dominic moved to the next seat to make way for the Prince to sit beside me. Susie and Laurent had quietly tucked in behind us and to my surprise Max and a handcuffed Yeuw, took their places a few rows back. The service was brief during which the priest asked those present and the Lord God to forgive the departed souls for their many sins. I felt no sense of loss, just relief when it was all over.

For the first time since I had arrived in Singapore I was grateful for the heat which enveloped us as we stepped outside. Then I was aware of Max coming towards me and could see Yeuw standing between two uniformed officers a few yards away.

"Joanna, would you be willing to speak to Yeuw? He has been extremely helpful in assisting us with our investigations and I see no reason to deny him this request." Max's face was serious. "He has been charged with accessory to murder, by the way."

I looked over Max's shoulder to the pleading face of the gorilla. Somehow I had never once felt that he had meant me any harm, in fact in his naive fashion he had only ever tried to protect me. But then my mind flashed back to the way he had joined in the 'fun' during my migraine attack! I looked away from him and reached for Dominic's hand.

"I don't know, Max, now is not the right time." Dominic gently squeezed my hand. "Tell Yeuw that I will come and visit him tomorrow morning."

I watched Max return to the waiting group, saw the disappointment in Yeuw's face and then the smile of acknowledgement.

"Come, I have booked a small room at the Hilton for a private lunch." Hussein had taken my arm and was steering myself and Dominic towards a waiting limousine. "You must come too!" he called to the surprised Laurent and Susie.

That afternoon Dominic took me to visit the university campus and in particular their massive library. He proudly produced a number of history books and thesis he had written on Malaysian culture and philosophy. I cannot deny that I was impressed. I had always thought that the young marine I had known all those years ago had had enormous potential. Nevertheless, I was constantly being astounded by the talents of this man. Of course he loved being praised and complimented, that hadn't changed one bit. Thankfully though, he had dropped the habit of admiring himself in every mirror and shop window as we passed. I slipped my arm through his and hugged it, he smiled that melting smile and decided it was time to go. Where was he going to take me next? Well, to the jewellers of course!

There we were, like a couple of teenagers trying on rings. Dominic never intended wearing one mind, he was just humouring me. He insisted that I have a huge diamond, but after nearly half an hours toing and froing, I realised that I did not really want an engagement ring, I would be perfectly happy with a simple gold wedding band when we eventually got married. To the frustration of the jeweller we left without buying a thing!

"You must be mad!" Susie was wailing over pre-dinner drinks in the sitting room. "Of course you must have an engagement ring. We'll go back tomorrow morning and choose one and we can find you a wedding dress at the same time!" "That is the last thing I want to do tomorrow Susie." I said firmly. "I am going to visit Yeuw in the morning and then we'll be packing and leaving for Malacca in the afternoon. "Perhaps we can have a shopping day in England, how does that sound?"

"Ooh, yes. Shopping in London, how exciting!" Susie did a couple of twirls sending a small wave of gin and tonic over the carpet. "Whoops, sorry! I'll get a cloth!"

"You've made a young woman very happy, Joanna." Dominic put his strong arm around my shoulder and cupped my chin in his bronzed hand. He kissed me slowly but gently on the lips and then held me close in silence for a full minute. Waves of sheer happiness filled my chest and tears sprung into my eyes. If there was a God and I had my doubts, he had been very very good to me.

Mrs Lee had done us proud. She had prepared a delicious stilton soup followed by vegetable moussaka, and then a glorious strawberry Pavlova. I felt absolutely stuffed and dreaded the thought of standing on the scales when I got back to England. The Pavlova was apparently Dominic's absolute favourite and he downed two helpings. Despite the bloatedness, he still managed to find an enormous amount of energy for making love later that night!

When I entered the interview room the following morning, Yeuw was already seated on the opposite side of a small table. Two armed guards stood to attention against the wall behind him. Dominic had gone to join Max and Laurent for a coffee so that my meeting with Yeuw could be a little more personal, if not completely alone.

"Please to sit down, Miss Joanna. I thank you for coming." I sat down on the hard wooden chair and looked across at the gorilla who was now squeezed into grey prison clothes that consisted of matching cotton T-shirt and elasticated trousers. His wrists were still handcuffed in front and I could not help but notice that the fingernails on his huge hands had been bitten down almost to the quicks.

"We can speak freely, Miss Joanna, these guards do not have English. This is good because what I have to say will surprise you and is not for their ears." His tone was strangely cold and I sensed that he had something on his mind that he was keen to unload. He continued. "Before the Prince and I went to England, I was happy. I have a home and a future wife. Your Father, he tell me I was like his son and I was glad. Now they are all dead, I have nothing and you are to blame."

"But Yeuw, I did not ask the Prince to find me and I certainly did not expect all these terrible things to happen." I could not see where this conversation was leading, Yeuw had bowed his head and now took a very deep long breath.

"You must understand Miss Joanna, I have to avenge their deaths and this is the only way I know how."

Then as if in slow motion, I watched him rise from his chair and swing his clenched handcuffed fists in a full circle into the face of one of the guards. The second guard stood stock still in shock and before he could react the man's head had been smashed against the stone wall. I rose from my chair and turned towards the door opening my month to scream but was too late. The mighty arms were around my neck and were dragging me backwards across the table. I clawed at his hands and kicked as hard as I could with my heels against his calves, but the vice began to tighten on my neck and the pressure began to build in my face and head. "Please, Yeuw, please let me go!" I gasped. "No, Miss Joanna, I will kill you if you do not stop struggling. You are my hostage, they will let me leave if I have you captive." He relaxed his hold just a little.

I stopped struggling and fought for some air. "Please Yeuw, they will not let you go, you must see that. You will only make things much worse for yourself."

"Knock on the door and tell them that you are ready to leave." He carried me to the door and shook me like a rag doll. "Do it!" he hissed.

With my head still held in a vice I reached out, tapped the door and told the guard outside to unlock it. The door opened and the startled guard immediately drew his hand gun. He shouted at Yeuw in Chinese only to throw the gun to the ground after Yeuw's angry response. Half dragging and half carrying me, Yeuw lumbered down the corridor, up a flight of stairs and through swing doors into a large open plan office full of uniformed officers. Yeuw shouted out commands in Chinese and the officers stood back to let us through. Now I was getting angry, I was not afraid of Yeuw, I still did not believe that he had any real intention of killing me. But he was bloody well hurting my neck. I felt for one of his hands and grasped his thumb. With all the strength I could find I started to prise it away from my throat and then bend it back. I heard Yeuw gasp and I then used both hands to force his thumb back at a most alarming angle. He yelled and released his grip just enough for me to slip my head out from under his arm. I held firmly onto that thumb and to my delight my action was disabling him. A rush of black uniforms had surrounded us and the gorilla was being overpowered, desks and chairs were crashing to the ground, it was as if a poltergeist was in the room. At last the great man lay prostrate on his stomach like a floundering whale, with at least eight officers pinning him down.

A female officer was sitting me in a chair and handing me a glass of water. "You certainly found his Achilles heel." She was smiling and speaking in perfect English. "In his case his Achilles thumb!"

I found myself smiling back, I had actually come out the victor all by myself for once. "Would you like me to get your husband?" She had sat beside me and was looking intently at my neck. "You're going to have a few bruises there I'm afraid." "I'm fine thank you. I just need to retrieve my bag from the interview room." I sighed.

Nipping into the ladies loo with my bag I brushed my hair and touched up my makeup.

"High, guys!" I smiled, when I finally found the coffee drinking trio. "All done, time to go!" "Did everything go all right with Yeuw?" asked Max. "Oh, yes." I smiled. "I sorted him out alright and before I left I gave him the thumbs up." The men looked at me as if I was perhaps on something strange and rose from their chairs.

"Laurent is flying back to Singapore tonight with Max and will join us on our flight to England on Monday" Dominic smiled. "Are you all right Joanna, you look a little flushed." "Yes, yes I'm fine." I lied lifting the collar of my shirt a little higher around my neck, which was starting to throb. "So, we'll see you on Monday Laurent and hopefully you too Max before we leave for England."

"You certainly will." Promised Max who was being approached by the female officer I had met earlier.

"Come on Dominic time to get back, packing and things, you know!" I prompted and headed for the door with Dominic in my wake.

"Why are you in such a hurry, Joanna?" asked a perplexed Dominic as we got outside. I shaded my eyes and looked up and down the street. "Where is the nearest bar?" I asked. "You can buy me a nice cool beer and I will tell you all about it!"

Chapter 30

"I daren't let you out of my sight for one minute Joanna, my god, if I had had any inkling that you might be in danger, I would never have left you alone with him!" Dominic's arm was around my shoulder in a corner seat of the lounge bar at the Hilton. I had swallowed a beer in one and was halfway through a second.

"For god's sake, how could anyone imagine that Yeuw could overpower two armed guards?" I said, shaking my head. "It was a final bid for freedom of course, damned foolish but you can't blame the man for trying. I feel strangely sorry for him, I can't explain why, but I do."

"I think I understand, darling." Dominic smiled sympathetically. "Yeuw was always going to be a victim, easily led and desperate to belong. Well, he's found himself a permanent home now, that's for sure." In silence we finished our drinks and then decided to head for home.

Back in my room I lay on the bed and dosed for an hour. Dominic needed to organise a number of things with the men and Mrs Lee. Vic was to travel with us in the Wrangler Jeep and would return to KL once we were finally deposited in Singapore, taking the vehicle back with him. I was going to miss this place and despite my longing to return home and be with Dippy, I had quite a lump in my throat. We still had Abdul's funeral to attend in the morning, which was going to be a terribly sad affair. Again, with my eyes closed, I could see the murdered man's grey agonised face turning slowly towards me, with its fixed silent scream and staring eyes. I shuddered and sat up on the bed. I would have a soak in the bath and then pack. We were intending to leave by four O'clock and it made sense to get on with the packing as soon as possible.

Susie was just coming out of the bathroom as I crossed the landing. She could not hide her excitement and dragged me into her room to show me all the clothes she had strewn across the bed. "Do you not have any warm clothes?" I asked, thinking of the unpredictability of English Summers.

"Well, only skiing clothes, I suppose some of my snow outfits might do." She produced a huge red padded jacket, which would probably take up most of the space in the Jeep. Quickly rummaging through her wardrobe I found a lightweight waterproof jacket, a sweater and a couple of pairs of trousers. Also walking boots and socks.

"Now you're only visiting for two weeks, Susie, I would suggest you reduce your packing by half." Oh dear, I was sounding an awful lot like a mother, but Susie didn't seem to mind in the slightest. She just gave me a huge hug and then bursting into song skipped around the room throwing all sorts of things back into drawers and taking other items out. Bursting with pleasure at her obvious happiness, I closed the door quietly behind me and headed for the bathroom. The lovely deep luxurious bath eased any remaining tenseness and at last I was ready for packing and the start of my return journey.

We arrived in Malacca after dark and headed straight for our adjoining rooms at the same club that Dominic and I had stayed in on the outward journey. Susie and I were sharing a twin room and Vic and Dominic the adjoining one. This arrangement was for safety reasons as it was perfectly possible for members of Cord's murdering cronies to still be at large. The adjoining door remained open all night and thankfully we all enjoyed eight hours uninterrupted sleep. By now I had grown accustomed to the humidity and would find it quite strange to be back in the clear cool air in Devon.

Before leaving Dominic's house, I had called him into the study for a very important reason. I wanted Margaret to have the rubies and diamonds that were still carefully stored in his safe. Dominic was unsure about it, they had to be worth a fortune possibly millions! But I had been insistent, I wanted Margaret and her family to be able to find a safe secure place to live with no expenses spared. He had given in when he realised how very important this was to me and he agreed to take the gems with us.

The funeral was taking place in the city centre mosque, followed by a small reception at Margaret's home in the suburbs. Abdul's family was quite large and relatives had travelled from all over Malaysia to attend. We took our place at the rear of the mosque sitting cross legged on the faded eastern carpet for over two hours. At last the entourage wound its way out of the building down the wide stone steps to a large paved courtyard. Here Margaret and her family greeted friends and relatives bowing, kissing and clenching hands. From the top of the steps I could see the Commander sitting a few yards away in the shade, on what appeared to be a shooting stick. He acknowledged my wave and beckoned us to join him.

"She is doing well, I think." He smiled and nodded in Margaret's direction. "Financially though, she is going to have problems. I will help as much as I can but my own financial position, beyond my naval pension, is not too good. Too many years of playing bridge I'm afraid."

"Commander, I have made provision for Margaret, but it involves a substantial settlement and I will need your help in making the arrangements." Lowering my voice I told him about the gems and that we had them with us.

"My dear, this is wonderful news. But I am afraid that my health is not too good and my doctor has instructed me to return to my home in Singapore as soon as possible." He thought for a moment. "I must let my wife in on the secret, she is a good woman and will see to it that Margaret is looked after should anything happen to me. She is ten years younger and is still in good health."

"We'll take the gems with us to Singapore and deposit them with your bank." Dominic whispered. "I have a friend who is in the trade and will give you an honest price for them."

"Commander, I want you to keep 25% of the proceeds." I said, taking his hand. "Without you Abdul and his family may not have survived this long and the last thing they would want is for you to have to give up bridge playing at your time of life!"

"Oh, my dear. I don't know what to say." The old man lifted his white cotton hat and bowed his head. "I just cannot tell you how grateful I am."

We all looked up at the sound of footsteps and Margaret joined us in the shade. "Miss Joanna, you come." I took her outstretched hands and standing on her tiptoes she kissed both my cheeks. A flurry of Malay ensued and Dominic explained that she wanted me to travel with her and her children to her house, the Commander would join Dominic, Susie and Vic in the Jeep. For the whole of the ten minute taxi ride Margaret held my hand with the occasional little squeeze and sad flickering smile. On reaching our destination, her eldest daughter ran into the tiny house in the midst of its productive vegetable garden to announce our arrival.

It may sound a little selfish, but I was glad to take our leave just over an hour later. What with the heat and the overcrowded house I felt in need of some peace and solitude. We returned to our rooms and collected our bags intending to head out for Singapore without delay. I really wanted to be on the move, a feeling of urgency had overtaken me. Susie and I sat in the back seat and it wasn't long before she was dozing with her head on my shoulder. I was immensely tired myself but would not be relaxed until the gems were safely in the Commander's bank deposit in Singapore. Both Dominic and Vic were carrying revolvers and they were well prepared and capable of handling any sudden attack. The bulk of the route back was in fact fast duel carriageway. Dominic stopped once for a natural break and some bottled water, but otherwise we made haste for our destination.

At last to my immense relief, I recognised the run up to the Causeway, which would take us across from Malaya onto Singapore Island. "Are we there yet?" A sleepy Susie stirred from her semi-foetal position, which she had taken an hour ago with her head on a rucksack.

"Just about to cross the Causeway," Dominic called from the driver's seat. "Can we call in and see Grandma?" Susie pulled herself forward and popped her head through between the two front seats. "In the morning sweetheart, let's get rid of these gems first and then find a long cool beer." Dominic said.

"I'll drink to that mate." Vic gave Dominic the thumbs up and the Jeep sped with renewed vigour over the Causeway and back into the great city of Singapore.

Dominic kept the engine running outside of the Hong Kong and Shanghai Bank, whilst Vic and I went in with the gems. At the enquiries desk we were directed to a waiting room from where we would be taken down to the safe deposit boxes below. The Commander had sent instructions that morning for the bank to expect me. A young Chinese bank official wearing a badge marked assistant manager, escorted by an armed guard, arrived almost immediately, bowed and took us through an adjoining door. At the bottom of a flight of marble stairs, he placed a key into the lock of a giant steel door and the armed guard did the same in an adjacent lock. The door hissed and slowly opened.

We passed through the open doorway, past a seated guard and through another identical door, which was opened in the same way. At last we entered the safe deposit room where rows of slim metal drawers covered the walls from floor to ceiling. The assistant manager directed me to a table and chair where he asked me to sign a well-thumbed register. He asked for proof of identity, so I offered my passport. Satisfied he produced a plastic card from his pocket, handed it to me, walked over to one of the metal drawers and pointed at the slot for the card. He placed a second card into an adjacent slot and then removed it.

"We will leave you now, Miss Wilde. Please ring this bell when you have finished."

Left alone in the claustrophobic atmosphere of the metal room, I hastily placed the card in the slot, a clicking sound ensued and then the drawer slid silently open. Without hesitation I removed the velvet bag containing the gems from my travel bag, took one last look inside and placed it in the drawer.

"Wait a minute, Joanna," Vic held my arm. "I have no doubt that this is the Commander's drawer, but let's just check to see if there is anything else in it that will give us proof." I nodded. "Good thinking, Vic." Reaching for the step ladder designed for this purpose, I climbed up so that I could see clearly into the drawer. To my relief a large brown envelope lay on top of a pile of documents and it read: 'Last Will and Testament - Commander Paul C Bennett.' "It's the right drawer, Vic. Let's go"

Vic rang the bell and seconds later the door slid open, we stepped through. I felt the hairs prickle on the back of my neck. A gun barrel was just inches from my face! "Hold it right there, put your hands on your heads." The voice was Scottish and male. Vic turned slowly with his hands on his head until he was facing in the same direction as myself. The guard moved the barrel of his hand gun until it was two inches from Vic's temple. "OK sergeant, stand at ease!" "Robbo, you bastard you nearly gave me a bloody heart attack, what the hell are you doing here?" Vic spluttered. "Came back to the island last year, got this job in security. It's great to see you mate and who is this lovely lady?" The red faced, ginger haired ex-Marine grinned widely in my direction. With my heart still having palpitations, I held my hand up to stop the conversation deteriorating any further and reminded Vic that this was not the time and place for renewing old acquaintances. The old comrades agreed to meet that evening and with a sigh of relief I at last found myself back in the Jeep.

"Everything all right?" asked Dominic "You were rather a long time."

"Yes, all done and dusted." I smiled. "Now please let's get to Mickey and Julie's house; I'm in desperate need of a cold shower!"

Chapter 31

"Mother, Mother Joanna is here!" Fourteen year old Tam was holding the door open and shouting excitedly for her mother. Julie came rushing out as fast as her tiny feet and high cork shoes could carry her. "Oh, Joanna, welcome back. Come in, come in!"

Dominic's frame had filled the doorway behind me and Julie's face immediately took on a school marm expression. "I understand you are also staying Mr Francis. As you are engaged to Joanna, I have assumed that you will be sharing her room." Julie sounded just like a front of house hotelier. I could not help but laugh. "Please Julie, Dominic is not the awful person you think he is, are you darling."

Dominic stepped forward, bowed deeply and took Julie's tiny hand in his mighty one. He kissed it very gently and apologised profusely for his unforgivable behaviour when he had last been to the house. Then from behind his back he produced the fresh red roses we had collected especially for this purpose. Sweet Julie blushed and covered her open mouth with her hand. Taking the deep red flowers she then bowed low and smiled rather sheepishly.

"Thank you Mr Francis you are definitely forgiven, perhaps you would care to join me for a cool drink - a beer perhaps?"

"You took the words right out of my mouth Julie and please do call me Dominic." Then offering his arm to the flushed hostess, he escorted her through to the kitchen leaving Susie and I with the bags in the hallway.

Fifteen minutes later I had dragged the bags to our room and hung up most of our clothes. I gratefully slipped out of my rather sweaty crumpled outfit and stepped into a wonderfully cool shower.

"Well, well, lovely lady is there room for two?" This time it was me who dragged Dominic into the shower, he barely had time to shed his shirt and shorts!

A little later, nicely exhausted we lay dried, powdered and naked on the bed. "Do you know, darling, I think we've got that position in the shower just right." Dominic stretched, sighed and put his hands behind his head. "Of course, my being tall, strong and athletic makes all the difference.   Most men couldn't possibly achieve what I'm capable of when it comes to making love."

"Of course not darling" I whispered snuggling a little closer. "Mind you most men wouldn't get invited into my shower in the first place." "I think you meant to say *all* men, other than myself, Joanna." He rolled over onto his side and faced me.

"I wouldn't say that" I grinned, lightly running my forefinger along his bottom lip, "there's Robert Redford for a start....."

Back on the bed after the second cool shower he asked me if there was anyone else, other than Robert Redford, who I might invite into my shower. So I told him about Dippy, but that we usually showered under the hosepipe in the garden.

It was gone 9 o'clock in the evening and the third shower had made us late for dinner. The children had already dined with Susie and had taken her to the television room for the evening. Micky had arrived an hour earlier and looked relaxed in open neck white shirt and cream trousers. Julie had obviously told him about the 'new improved' Dominic and he rushed forward to greet us both enthusiastically.

"We have champagne on ice to celebrate your engagement!" he gushed. "Jimmy and Diane have also sent a telegram and wish to join us in raising our glasses to you both." With smiles all round we did that very thing and then sat down to a delicious chow mien and egg fried rice.

We slept liked logs that night and woke to a brand new day, knowing that we could relax like tourists until Monday.

"So what would my lovely fiancé like to do on a Saturday in Singapore?" Dominic stretched and threw back the sheet. "Anything as long as it's with you."

I sighed.

"We should consider Susie, I suppose, or just let her loose in the shopping centre."

Dominic chuckled.

"Why don't we all go and visit Chor Ling, take her the news" I suggested. "I'd also like to see the rest of her photograph album." "Yes, I was a little rude last time we were there, wasn't I." Dominic put his hands behind his head. "I was reluctant to have you see pictures of Susie's mother."

"That was perfectly understandable in the circumstances, darling. But I'd be interested to know more about her, but only if you don't mind talking about it." I snuggled closer to the naked Dominic and pulled the sheet around us.

"I met her in the library, here in Singapore," he began. *"Having decided to settle here I started to read up on the history of Malaysia and spent lunchtimes and often evenings in the reference library. Sue Ling was studying Politics and Economics. We found ourselves regularly sharing the same table and one day, as she was about to leave I asked her to join me for a drink. The drink became dinner and I finally drove her home at two O'clock in the morning. I found her fascinating, beautiful, her English was good and she was very entertaining company. I found out about her Communist activities much later."*

"Communist activities?" I asked, rather surprised.

"Yes, she was very interested in my military background and wanted me to meet with her university friends. All were studying politics and were involved in Communist activities. These included protest marches and some rather less friendly activities. By this time she was pregnant and not too happy about it. We married a month before Susie was born and moved in with Chor Ling, whilst looking for somewhere more suitable to live.

Meanwhile, I had a full time job as works manager for one of the larger electronics companies. By the time I was 30 I was made a Director and had bought a house. I was spending more and more time travelling, doing deals on behalf of the company and myself. Unbeknown to me, Sue Ling had secretly been

planning to attack a munitions depot in Malaya. She and her colleagues were
shot dead before they could make their escape. Susie was just five years old."

"Oh, Dominic." I gasped and pulled myself up into a sitting position. "You must
have been devastated and poor Susie."

"Susie spent most of her time with Chor Ling, she didn't see much of her mother.
Sue was much more interested in her political aspirations, I don't think she should
ever have been a mother."

"Did you love her very much?" I rested my head on his shoulder and hugged his
upper arm. "I loved her, but I don't think I was ever 'in love' with her." He
looked down at me with his warm smile and twinkling eyes. "Now I can tell the
difference because I am 'in love' with you." "Time for a cold shower." I grinned.

Chor Ling was over the moon to see us and with the hand woven bedspread
we had chosen for her new apartment. She was very pleased to be on the third
floor and not too close to the noise at ground level. The one bed-roomed
accommodation was, to me, terribly cramped but compared with her previous
home very spacious. She loved her little kitchenette, the separate bedroom and
the bathroom with running hot water. She had a television in the corner of her
still rather empty sitting room and excitedly showed us how it worked. There
was room for two chairs on her tiny balcony and a little table in between. She
had also managed to squeeze in a number of her beloved jungle plants in pots.
We all agreed that it was very nice indeed and that we should celebrate by going
out to lunch. We would then go and find her a nice big comfortable armchair to
place in front of her television. Altogether that weekend went wonderfully well.
Susie stayed overnight with Chor Ling and Dominic and I at last enjoyed our
romantic dinner together, at Raffles! We chose a table far away from the one I
had shared with Laurent, and had a fabulous time.

On the Monday we joined Laurent for the 10 O'clock flight out of
Singapore on the first leg of our journey back to England. I felt incredibly
exhausted, less than three weeks away from home seemed like a lifetime, I

couldn't wait to see Dippy again.

Before leaving Micky and Diane's house and inviting them to come and stay with me in Devon, I had rung Emma. For once she actually listened, probably in a slight state of shock when I told her that Dominic and I were engaged and that he and his daughter were coming home with me. In her usual endearing way she still managed to have the last say and to take my thunder away by announcing that she was pregnant! I still held back the news that Dominic was actually her father as I felt this should wait until we were face to face. Dominic had arranged to hire a four wheel drive vehicle for the fortnight, which would be waiting for us at Heathrow. The plan was to drop me off at the top of my lane and for Dominic and Susie to come back half an hour later. This way I could make the announcement before Emma came face to face with her father for the first time. Emma had always accepted her fatherless upbringing, she had only brought the subject up once and was happy with my explanation. She seemed quite content not to be sharing me with anyone else and did her best to put off any potential boyfriend who expressed more than a passing interest in me. But then, I did nothing to stop her anyway and gave almost all of my attention to the success of the business - and her. But things were different now, she was married with a baby on the way. At last any responsibility I still felt for her, could be described purely as a mother's love for her grown up child. I could now look forward to a very happy future with the only man I had ever loved, possibly write a book and be at peace with myself.

The flights were reasonably uneventful and we arrived at Heathrow at just after four o'clock, which meant that without any hold ups we could be in Devon by seven thirty in the evening. Dominic drove the first half of the way and I did the second half. As we passed over the border from Somerset into Devon, on the M5, I felt my spirits lift and Dominic was snoring loudly. Susie squealed a lot at the site of cows, sheep, thatched cottages, old pubs and in fact at everything. We came off the motorway at the Tiverton junction and now I was really feeling back home. Through Bickleigh and up into the hills to the village of Cadeleigh. I pulled into the pub car-park at 7.25 and woke Dominic intending to swap seats with him. He jumped back into consciousness and at the sight of the pub slid out of his seat and walked trance like through the door marked lounge bar. We had no alternative but to follow him in!

That first glass of real ale was absolutely delicious. Dominic could not believe the improvement in the beer and the amazing choice. After he had tasted a second pint of a different ale, I had no choice but to drag him physically back to the vehicle so he could drop me down to the farmhouse. I stepped onto the single track road at the top of my lane and waved Dominic and Susie out of sight as they enthusiastically headed back to the pub. I stood for a few minutes in the silence of my most favourite spot in the world, breathing in the smell of new mown hay. It was very much the month of August in Devon, the lack of rain had resulted in dried out hedgerows and scorched brown grass. My feet kicked up small clouds of dust as I walked down my lane towards the house and then I heard Dippy barking. He knew someone was coming, did he know it was me? Then to my utmost pleasure around the bend at the bottom of the lane came Finny, the rush of greyness and speed of this gorgeous lurcher brought tears to my eyes. I stopped dead in my tracks waiting for the impact and then saw Dippy struggling in Finny's wake trying to keep up. Rather than be thrown to the ground, I decided to sit down. Then Finny was on me, crazily licking, bouncing and wriggling. Dippy at last made it and his lovely warm black body was in my arms, wriggling with pleasure from head to toe and licking the whole of my face like there was no tomorrow! "Oh Dippy boy, how I have missed you." I looked into those beautiful brown moist eyes and hugged him again as he snuggled up as close as he possibly could beside me.

Finny had rushed back down the lane to announce my arrival and by the time Dippy and I had reached the gate in the ivy covered wall, Emma was rushing through it. A big hug was followed typically by the question. "Just look at the state of you Mother, you look as if you have been rolling around in the dirt!" Then looking over my shoulder in the direction from whence I had come she frowned and asked. "So where is the big white hunter and his daughter?" "They've stopped off at the pub and will be here in half an hour or so." I smiled a little nervously.

"Hey, Mum!" The cheeky Harry was waving me towards the conservatory door. "Cold beers are ready and waiting!"

Chapter 32

"Well, he's a fine one I must say!" Emma was sounding very proper. "Fancy giving the pub priority over meeting me!"

We had taken our beers through the conservatory and out onto the flag stoned area where I kept a permanent outdoor seat. We sat high above a typical deep Devon valley with patchwork hills rolling away into the far distance. It was so good to be back home.

"Emma, darling, I wanted to talk to you before Dominic and Susie arrived." I smiled nervously and took her hand. For once she remained quiet, sensing some importance in what I was about to say.

"Do you remember when you were about twelve, you asked me about your Father and I told you that he had gone to Singapore and never returned?" I asked softly. "Yes, of course I do. But why are you bringing that subject up now?" Emma looked uncomfortable and took her hand out from under mine. She shifted her gaze to the view and sighed deeply.

"His name was Dominic Francis. I never really stopped loving him, but as the years rolled on I gave up all hope of ever seeing him again." I took her hand again. "When I arrived in Singapore I had the shock of my life, Dominic the Great White Hunter and my guide, turned out to be none other than Dominic Francis. Do you understand what I am saying, Emma, the Dominic I have brought home with me is your father!"

Emma's jaw had dropped and she had paled beyond recognition. Then my worst fears erupted as she snatched her hand away and rose to her feet. Her chair fell awkwardly to the side and Finny leapt up in shock. Dippy rose to a sitting position and began to pant nervously. Her pale face began to redden and at last she found her voice. "Are you absolutely mad, he deserted you - and me - how could you mother, how could you bring that man back into our lives?"

Harry rose and put his arms around her but she pushed him away. "Don't treat me like a child, how do you expect me to react!"

"Perhaps you should let Joanna tell you the whole story, darling." Harry drew her down beside him but he could not prevent the tears from falling.

"Emma darling, your grandfather had lied to me and covered up the truth of the situation." I took a swallow of beer. "Dominic did not desert us, George Worme told him that I had aborted you, a terrible thing to do. A quarter of a century of potential happiness as a family was destroyed just to satisfy my father's evil selfishness."

"My God, the bastard," Harry gasped. He shook his head and smoothed Emma's dark auburn hair. "Did you hear what Joanna just said, Emma, your father didn't even know you were alive!"

I found a crumpled tissue in my pocket and passed it to my beautiful daughter. She gave her nose a good hard blow and looked at me through her wet glistening lashes. The blueness of her eyes had been exaggerated by the tears and a great lump came into my throat.

"My father is a quarter of a mile away at the pub, with my sister! It's unbelievable." Emma rose again and taking a deep breath announced that 'she had better go and tidy herself up and get up the pub then.'

Emma had been up in her room for five minutes when my mobile rang, it was Susie. "Joanna, I think we may have a problem. Dominic has just started a fifth pint of ale and I don't think he's capable of driving! He's got into conversation with some of the local men and they are egging him on. I've told him that we need to leave but he keeps laughing at me and telling me not to worry. It's so embarrassing, I think he may be too drunk to meet Emma!" "Well, if he is in that sort of state then we may as well come and join you. The sooner Emma has a few drinks inside her the better!"

Emma was ready to go and I could tell that she had given herself a good talking to. I told her that Dominic may be a bit worse for wear, which Harry thought was hilarious. We piled into the red jeep, with Dippy and Finny in the back, and headed up the lane to the road. The pub car-park was quite full, the hire vehicle looked blocked in and we just managed to tuck in as someone was leaving. I entered the lounge bar with Emma and Harry in my wake and a very relieved Susie rushed towards us.

"Oh Joanna, I'm so sorry," she shouted over the noise of the bar conversation. "I just can't get him off the bar stool!"

I spotted a corner table, which was just being vacated and steered us all towards it. Away from the crowd I was at least able to introduce the two sisters. Emma was very formal and held out her hand, but Susie being Susie, flung her arms around her sibling with such enthusiasm that the table rocked. Gushing with excitement she told Emma how she had always longed for a sister and now she was the luckiest girl in the world. Emma was initially struck dumb by the overwhelming presence of this lovely half Malayan young woman with her long golden hair and blue twinkling eyes. I winked at Harry and motioned him in the direction of the bar. "Harry and I will get some drinks." I think the girls heard me, but by then they were both deep in conversation and a flicker of a smile was actually tickling Emma's lips.

"I think Susie has won Emma over already!" smiled Harry. "One down and one to go!"

I nodded and squeezed through the crowd to see the blond head of Dominic holding audience with a bunch of complete strangers on bar stools. Catching sight of me, he stood up, towering above his neighbours and opened his arms whacking some poor fellow's beer arm in the process. "Hey, watch it you clumsy idiot!" The man spat angrily at Dominic.

"Sorry mate, let me buy you another one." The drunken Dominic flung his arm around the man's shoulder. "Tell you what, I'm celebrating and this is my lovely fiancée. Drinks all round!"

An almighty roar of approval reverberated around the pub and people seemed to come out of the woodwork. Harry laughed loudly. "He's all right your man. What's he like sober?"

An hour later new friends were helping to get Dominic into the passenger seat of the four wheel drive vehicle. Needless to say, Emma was not impressed but had been persuaded by Susie that this was an isolated incident and that Dominic was unused to the strength of the British beer. They were already firm friends and I could still hear them talking downstairs long after the rest of us had gone to bed.

As you can imagine Dominic felt very ill in the morning. He had yet to meet Emma properly and remained in bed until gone eleven. Finally, after a long cool shower and several cups of coffee he emerged into the sunlight in dark glasses and baseball cap. Emma and Susie were not back yet from a long walk over Visitors Hill with the dogs and Harry had driven into Tiverton for some fresh supplies. I had washed and hung out the dirty washing on the line and was wandering back from a stroll round the pond when I saw Dominic, head down, emerging from the conservatory door.

"I thought you had all deserted me." He croaked, sounding like a small boy with a dry throat. "We would never do that, Dominic, although I was sorely tempted last night." I said teasingly.

"It was the real ale, my god it's strong." he groaned putting his hand on the top of his head and slowly sinking into one of the chairs next to the old garden table, under the pergola. I sat down with him and rested my hand over his. "Emma and Susie are getting on really well, it's just wonderful. I had serious concerns as to how well Emma would take the news, but she seems to be loving it, mind you we must thank Susie for that - she's irresistible!"

Dominic attempted to laugh then winced at a sudden pain in the top of his head. "You're right, of course, she charms everyone and in particular her dad!" I felt his hand tighten on mine as the gate opened and Finny, followed by Dippy, rushed through. I warned Dominic to brace himself as Finny leapt for his lap.

"Don't be too flattered, that dog is anybody's." Emma was crossing the lawn towards us wearing baggy white shorts and purple vest. A wide brimmed floppy hat shaded her eyes and her slim feet were strapped into comfortable all terrain sandals. "Don't get up, I wouldn't want you keeling over on my behalf!" She was addressing the hung over Dominic who, sat with a lurcher on his lap, made quite an amusing spectacle.

"I'll get some tea, perhaps you could give me a hand Susie," I prompted. Susie whose arms were full of pink and red rhododendron cuttings nodded enthusiastically and followed me to the kitchen.

"You two seem to be getting on extremely well." I said happily. "It was a very good idea to bring you to England with me, I think you've done Emma a power of good."

"Oh, Joanna," she sighed. "She is so lucky to have had a mother to bring her up, but do you know, she also wanted a sister. Now we both have what we have always wanted and this place is just heaven. I think I might like to transfer my studies to England, what do you think?" "I don't think you should rush into anything Susie, after all you only arrived yesterday!" I laughed.

"Nevertheless, sometimes you get an instinct for what is meant to be." She sighed and gazed out through the open window where butterflies could be seen fluttering around the abundant honeysuckle. I followed her gaze and could only nod in silent agreement.

Susie carried the tray with my big pot of tea, milk, sugar and mugs. I followed behind with a plate of Emma's home-made shortbread. In the shade of the pergola, father and daughter were deep in conversation, I caught the end of Emma's conversation and smiled. "...and I expect you to take good care of her, she can be a bit dotty at times." Dominic roared with laughter and then clutched at his sore head.

"Emma has such a great sense of humour, darling" he was grinning painfully.

"Now just a minute, father." Emma quipped. "I'm being serious." "Of, course you are Emma, I wouldn't dare to think otherwise." And Dominic laughed again, setting Susie off. I looked at Emma's annoyed expression and couldn't help but join in the laughter. Poor Emma desperately tried to keep the status quo, but laughter is infectious and against her better judgement her chin started to quiver. "So what's the joke then?" Harry was struggling up the path with loaded shopping bags and the dogs were attempting to assist him. "There's plenty more of these in the Jeep." Dominic attempted to rise but sank immediately back into his seat. The girls rushed to assist, leaving Dominic and me to enjoy the tea.

Emma and Harry had just two days left of their holiday, during which they took us to visit the armoury at Bickleigh Castle where they had been married the previous week. We went to Exmouth and walked along the beach, calling in at the Rifleman's Inn for lunch. We drove past the Royal Marine Camp so that Susie could see where Dominic had been stationed and had an evening meal at Denleys in Topsham. On the Saturday morning Emma, Harry, Susie, Finny and their luggage squeezed into the red jeep, climbed up the dusty drive and headed for London. Susie had asked to spend the second week with Emma but we all knew that Laurent and London were the real attractions. Dominic, Dippy and I jogged behind them to the top of the lane and waved them off along the single track road. We walked back down the lane hand in hand with Dippy enthusiastically leading the way. I think that was one of the happiest moments of my life.

Over the next week, as promised, Dominic did clear the pond of overgrown weed and reeds. He cut the lawns and new pathways through the woods. We found another patch of brambled garden which, when cleared, unearthed an old wishing well which Dominic scrubbed and restored to working use. By the end of that second week I felt as if Dominic had always been there, in a way I suppose he always had been.

All packed and ready to go, Dominic and I clung to each other at the garden gate. He would be returning in a six weeks during which time I hoped to make great in roads into my first book. Dippy and I rode with him as far as the pub and walked back after feeling very sorry for ourselves over a large gin and tonic in the beer garden.

~~~~~~~~~~~~~~~~~~~~~~~~~~~~

So, you might think that my great adventure was over. I had retraced my father's last steps only to discover him still alive! Had found my lost love on the way and met some incredible new people. No, the adventure was about to be relived in my first novel, it was just beginning!

The following morning I woke late with Dippy snoring loudly at my side. After coffee we walked to the top of Visitor's hill and sat side by side in the long swaying dried grass. Dippy leant into me and I into him, this was truly heaven and I no longer carried a heavy heart. Inspired we jogged back down the hill and into the cool kitchen. I poured a large glass of white wine and took it into the study. I switched the computer on and read the record I had made of the Prince's visit. I was ready to write:

'And so it began...

Epilogue

The following spring, *Emma* gave birth to a bouncing baby boy and two years later a gorgeous baby girl. Her PR business went from strength to strength and she won the businesswoman of the year award in 1999. In 2003, Harry was head hunted by the golfing world and took a very well paid job managing three golf courses in Italy. With technology having become more sophisticated, Emma and the children moved out to join him and she now works successfully from her studio near Siena.

Susie stayed in London for two months, having a very exciting time. She and *Lauren* had a brief affair until Interpol sent him off to catch another criminal. She returned to Kuala Lumpur to finish her studies and became engaged to the very rich Honourable James Bowles whom she met on a university exchange visit to England.

The Commander survived another three years, having spent enormous sums of money at the card table, leaving behind his younger wife to live in luxury, on the coast of Singapore. Abdul's wife *Margaret* was able to buy homes for all their offspring and to fund a school in Malacca for disadvantaged children. She was to become a very important figure in local politics and Abdul would have been very proud of her.

Prince Hussein, found a 'deberatante' at a nightclub in London. He married and produced four children in quick succession. He built a large portfolio of worldwide real estate and became known as a very hard, shrewd businessman.

As for **Dominic and me**, did we eventually marry after years of flying backwards and forwards to each other's homes? Sadly, poor old **Dippy** went up to join the other doggies in the sky and I found the farmhouse unbearable without him. So I did eventually move to Kuala Lumpur, where **Satan** the golden retriever made me very welcome. We are now in the throes of searching for a second home near Emma in Tuscany and I am well into my third novel.

Oh, yes. I forgot to mention that three weeks after my father's second death, I received a letter from lawyers in Bolivia, South America. They were handling the substantial estate of the 'late **George Worme**' and, as I was the main beneficiary, would be grateful if I could arrange to attend the reading of the will as soon as possible. *However, that is another story.* Check out *'The Bolivian Connection'* on Amazon.

Footnote: *All of the locations, pubs, and restaurants in Devon existed in 1995 and most still do. They are all worth a visit and in particular, for drinking only, The Exeter Inn in Thorverton, near Exeter. Say hello to John for me.*

Made in the USA
Charleston, SC
24 March 2015